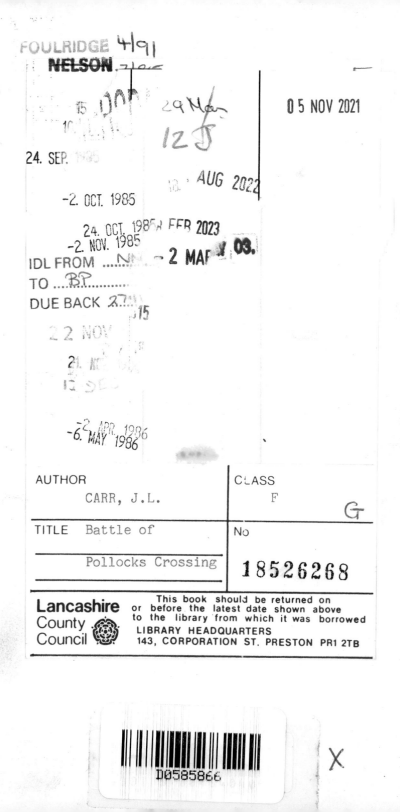

By the same author

A Day in Summer
A Season in Sinji
The Harpole Report
How Steeple Sinderby Wanderers Won the F.A. Cup
A Month in the Country

For Children

The Red Windcheater
The Flying House
The Old Cart
The Green Children of the Woods

THE BATTLE OF POLLOCKS CROSSING

J. L. Carr

VIKING

VIKING

Penguin Books Ltd, Harmondsworth, Middlesex, England
Viking Penguin Inc., 40 West 23rd Street, New York, New York 10010, U.S.A.
Penguin Books Australia Ltd, Ringwood, Victoria, Australia
Penguin Books Canada Ltd, 2801 John Street, Markham, Ontario, Canada L3R 1B4
Penguin Books (N.Z.) Ltd, 182–190 Wairau Road, Auckland 10, New Zealand

First published 1985

Typeset in VIP Baskerville

Typeset, printed and bound in Great Britain by
Hazell Watson & Viney Limited,
Member of the BPCC Group,
Aylesbury, Bucks

British Library Cataloguing in Publication Data

Carr, J.L.
The Battle of Pollocks Crossing.
I. Title
823'.914[F]   PR6053.A694

ISBN 0-670-80559-9

FOR C.M.
IN HIS
BASEMENT.
R. I. P.

What past can be yours, O journeying boy
   Towards a world unknown,
Who calmly, as if incurious quite
On all at stake, can undertake
   This plunge alone?

Thomas Hardy, 'Midnight on the Great Western'

Yet meet we shall, and part and meet again
Where dead men meet, on lips of living men.

Samuel Butler

'No, not if ten Vice-Presidents and each with two heads on his neck were coming to unveil it,' Mr Gidner said sourly. 'God willing – and I'm pretty sure he is – I never again shall set foot in your United States. Never!

'Guest of Honour? Honour! What has honour to do with Pollocks Crossing?

'And this monument you go on about! On a bucking bronco like Buffalo Bill? No? Just a State Tourist Commission cast-iron marker! Well, get the inscription right. What about this?

Henry Farewell & James Ardvaak
Hereabouts done to death
by their countrymen.
July 5th, 1930.
R.I.P.

'No? You don't think the folks back home in Palisades would like that? Well, I hardly suppose that they would. Even after fifty years, the shame can't have rubbed off. You're not enjoying this, are you? How old did you say you were? Eighteen! Just out of High School, eh? Becky Farewell was eighteen.

'I suppose they wanted to wheel me out like a museum piece. Well, they've wasted your air-fare.'

He gloomily poked the fire.

'But thanks for this tobacco. Very civil of you. Can't buy Prince Albert in Britain, let alone Bradford. I used to get it at Vogler's place on Oxbow. But Vogler must be dead long ago. Shot whilst hunting! Pheasants or humans?'

He scraped a sodden wad from his pipe bowl and flicked it into the flames.

*

On May 20th, 1929, George Gidner travelled by cheap day-excursion train to London and presented himself at the offices of the Anglo-American Goodwill League which, in those days, maintained itself in style on Berkeley Square. And when the character reference from his vicar and a testimonial to his professional competence grudgingly provided by a headmaster had been glanced at, his opinion was sought on the likely outcome of the County Cricket Championship and the improvident idleness of the urban labouring classes. His earnest replies did not challenge the dogma of the interviewing elderly canon and Boer War colonel and, when each took a turn at tediously elaborating these, his air of respectful attention much impressed them. So, confident that he felt no calling to change things from the way they were, both agreed that he was well, in fact unusually well, suited to represent England's youth in the United States of America. (And felt their judgement confirmed by his hard-wearing tweed suit, stout shoes, club tie and short-back-and-sides haircut.)

So it was no more than a ploy to improve the time until afternoon tea was served (without charge) in the members' withdrawing-room that caused the canon to ask why he wished to live and teach a twelvemonth in a foreign land. And George, having cleverly anticipated that this question was bound to be asked, uttered a prepared statement which boiled down to a belief that he would return a different man. (Though, of course, this was not his true reason.)

'A Different Man!' the colonel exclaimed. 'Different! Different! How Different? Why, what's wrong with you, man? Is there something you should have told us?'

But the tea-bell tinkled, so, with diminished confidence, they dismissed him to the converted wine-cellars where a clerk was employed to sort out the vexatious details of such transactions.

'You're overlate,' she cried peevishly. 'And you can forget anything that lah-di-dah bunch of fuddyduddies upstairs told you. All snapped up . . . New York City, Beverly Hills, all them pretty little Christmas-card spots in Vermont full of snow and churchgoers. The lot! Come back earlier next year.'

'Gone? Everything? You mean to tell me I've come all the way from Bradford for nowt. Then why didn't that pair of fatheads say so? They aren't giving away free tickets on the L.N.E.R. you know,' George exclaimed, regretting suppressed opinion of the colonel's inanities.

'Ah!' the clerk said, responding favourably to her echoed belief. 'So you're down from Lancashire where the Real People live. As is my hubby, the which he never ceases from drumming into me and the nippers. Well, now as you're upset, it just happens there is one job left. Not that you'd want it. Where? In the middle. Where else? Yes, dead in the middle. Personally I've never heard of the spot and it only springs to mind because it starts with an "M" (as does the hubby's middle name). And if you insist that I look (even though nobody in their right mind would want to go there), I expect I could put myself to a heap of bother to dig it out from wherever it is. But, as it happens, would you credit it, the first place I put my hand on!'

The single sheet read,

STATE	South Dakota.
CITY	Palisades.
SCHOOL	Grover Cleveland High.
GRADES	10 and 11.
COURSES	(a) American Literature.
	(b) Sentence Structuring.
COURSE BOOKS	(i) *A Treasury of our Native Bards*.
	(ii) Breitmeyer's *Sentence Diagramming Made Easy*.
CANDIDATE'S MOTIVATION	Wishes to effectivize his work ethic and advance career prospects by visiting English Literature Shrines.

George Gidner attentively studied this laconic document and measured himself against its requirements. 'Grades 10 and 11', 'sentence structuring', 'sentence diagramming' were a foreign language. Nor, but for the first twenty lines of *Hiawatha* an exacting grammar school master had made him learn, was he well up in the American bards. However, he turned from the clerk who was shuffling irritably and tried murmuring, 'South Dakota . . . California . . . Virginia . . . North Carolina . . . South Dakota'. He could make it sound no more than a drab 48th alternative. But, when he tested 'Palisades' against 'Macclesfield, Batley, Heckmondwyke, Stockport', that came off much better.

'I'll take the job,' he said.

'You are a darned sight too impulsive,' the woman replied crossly. 'And I bet that lot upstairs dodged telling you we won't tolerate our exchanges tripping gaily off, not stomaching what they find and belly-aching to be let slink home again. That very spot you now stand upon – we had such a one (except he was jumping for joy). Couldn't wait to be shipped there fast enough. "Alabama!" he kept squealing. You'd have thought he was off to Paradise. Within the calendar month . . . four weeks! . . . and we were getting a letter on every post whining that he'd come all over in spots and sores, had to line up with the blacks for free medication, hated his students (and they hated him) and could we please let him have an advance so he could buy a ticket home. Not a hope! We had his monicker on our disclaimer form. He's still there.'

'Above or below?' George asked drily and took the grudging little sheet near a window where, in better light, he discovered a message pencilled so faintly that he guessed his alter-ego, the distant Dakotan, must have feared some obstructive official might read it: 'I have heard tell that Europeans fear the Indian still roams the Plains. This is Not So.' From these words George guessed that his counterpart (whom he never was to meet) was as desperate to exchange Palisades for Somewhere Else as he was to escape from Bradford, and that he was puzzled and hurt because no one had hastened forward with a ticket of leave. And now, from the far-off prairie, it seemed that he could sense a faint throbbing noise, a sort of hum. So he returned to the counter and, pushing his face quite close to the clerk, said more loudly than he usually spoke, 'I shall take this job in South Dakota (which does not begin with an M): it sounds an exciting sort of spot. And depend upon it, I shall last my year out. Come what may.'

'Well, in that case, Good Luck to you,' the woman replied, taken aback by this stout affirmation. 'And I must say you look a big strong young chap (coming, as you do, from up where the Real People are) and I bet you didn't get that medal on your watch-chain for nothing neither. Whereas that Alabama man looked like a broken-down poet even before he set off. Sign your full name and state your next-of-kin (just in case). Well, we never know, do we? Also, state your religion so they'll know what to do with you (just in case, also). Now you're practically there. Easy, wasn't it?' She smiled encouragingly.

But, as he went off, she crowed to a hidden colleague, 'Wonders will never cease and that I'll declare on my dying day. That job in Cowtown, U.S.A. . . . . remember it? The one that's been gathering dust since Year Dot. I've got shot of it. To a big blue-eyed booby from up North. (Where the Real Folks live; ha!) Clever me!'

And, overhearing this, many years afterwards George Gidner admitted that the heart-beat from Palisades pulsed more faintly and that, by the time his train ran into Leeds Central (Up-Level) it was quite stilled.

One prediction was fulfilled immediately: he became Another Man.

The approaching journey obsessed him. On their weekly march to the public swimming-bath, he would halt his crocodiled class of children and leave it poised perilously beside the reeling tramcars whilst he slipped into the Carnegie Free Library to gaze at the tiny name, PALISADES, in Bartholomew's World Atlas. And his eye would trace the flow of the Bitter-root River which, rising by the springs of the Red River, poured itself into the Big Sioux River which then rolled off into the shifts and sandbars of the Missouri.

So this Palisades is a trading-post, he mused. And, when my students have restructured Breitmeyer's last set sentence of our day, in the cool of the evening, I shall stroll downalong the wharves and warehouses to watch river steamers breast the current, bound south or west (consulting the atlas) for Huron, Pierre, Shenandoah and remote fur stations, Sick Heart Pass and Long Delay and on and on to the far head-waters of the Yellowstone River.

His staffroom colleagues noticed this change.

'Mr Gidner seems sort of exalted since he landed that plush Yankee job,' Miss Dora Tippett said dejectedly to Mrs Bitterne (the cookery teacher) whose husband had just confirmed his promotion from shop-floor to under-management by going off with a nineteen-year-old filing-clerk.

'Exalted! What sort of a word is that!' Mrs Bitterne replied harshly. 'He just looks his usual oversized, flatfooted, futile self to me. What do you mean – "exalted"?'

'Well, sort of not himself. Starry-eyed. I sort of know he'll never come back to Balaclava Road Elementary any more. I sort of wish . . .'

But Miss Tippett did not feel it prudent to share her hopes and fears with Mrs Bitterne in her current frame of mind and only completed the sentence when, that night, she lay sleepless in her rented bed-sitter. 'I sort of wish I'd have gone to the pictures when he asked me last November. But he didn't seem much of a prospect when he was just himself. I sort of know he'll not date me again.' And she shed a tear.

She was right. Because he was saving up for the passage, George Gidner did not press his suit. But, although Dora Tippett withdraws from this story, it is no more than justice to say that his neglect was not because of her lack of charm, sort of. Far from it. As a matter of fact, at the tennis club that same summer, she met a rising young executive in a thread factory and married him.

That same August, George bought a Third Class ticket (for £18) on a transatlantic steamer sailing from Liverpool. His father closed his grocer's shop for the day and accompanied him to the dockside and, as the *Berengaria* drew away, called a last message. Because numerous other last messages thronged the air, George only imperfectly grasped his. But he felt pretty sure that it began, 'If you come across your mother's Uncle Braithwaite . . . give him your grandma's Whitby jet brooch . . .' However, what he shouted doesn't really matter: it has no significance in what happened later. Though the brooch has.

After four days of storm and sickness in cramped quarters, he reached the great city of New York. To nurse his straitened funds he did not linger but hastened through its heartless canyons to Penn Station. And thence to Chicago.

And that fabled city turned out to be just as cinema

films had testified. For he had sortied no more than a couple of blocks before a wailing black van sped towards him, stopped shudderingly and shot out four cops. Each held a hatchet. They galloped across the sidewalk and, shattering an unlocked door, tumbled into gloom. Then came an appalling row, unearthly wailing, doom thumps. George appealingly approached by-passers. But these, without pausing, shrank from him or roughly shouldered him aside. In fact, one man began to run quite rapidly backwards.

Then the murderous crew, in line and, perhaps, even in the same order, trotted out. They clattered into their van. Each sat bolt upright, gazing woodenly at his opposite. But, at the last moment, one, a fatherly man, took out his big red bandanna and, wiping first his chopper and then his moustache, turned and winked at George, whose terrified inclination was to bolt back to the railroad depot and hide. But then, recalling that a prime purpose of his long journey had been to observe and interpret the Americans' Way of Life, he bravely ventured to the wrecked doorway and peeped inside.

Behind the bar, an elderly bald-headed man, sole occupant of the battlefield, was not only alive but calmly wiping a tankard. Piled around him was a junk heap of savagely split gambling machines, springs and gears still twitching in terminal agony. One of these, trailing a ruptured intestinal cable, gamely struggled to its feet and, blazing spasmodic red and green signals, turned towards George who willed it to live. And, seeming to sense his concern, it spurted a few coins at his feet. But a bell chimed, lights fused in a puff of smoke; it slumped to the sawdust.

Only then, considering his prime duty was to present himself whole at Grover Cleveland High, did he retreat. For, as he reminded himself, what he had witnessed during this brief foray, merely confirmed that he could have Chicago explained by Edward G. Robinson any old evening and in a safe seat at his friendly Bradford cinema.

As he tracked back to the depot he was glad that this was not his journey's end. That lay an afternoon, evening and night ahead, across Illinois, Wisconsin, Minnesota, half Dakota. It would be different out there: life would have a primitive purity. Nevertheless, this savage scene deeply impressed him and he often (and tediously) cited it as an early awareness that violence was as American as oversweet apple-pie and tough buttermilk pancakes and would say, 'In its bizarre fashion, that Chicago tavern was the so-called Battle of Pollocks Crossing in miniature. Even a prophecy! Or a warning! When I reach that part of my story, you will see at once what I mean. But do not be alarmed: my sitting in this armchair is assurance that I survived it. Just.'

He found that leaving a great American city by rail was reassuringly like his vicar's forecast of the departure of one's untrammelled soul: one moment you were in the gay bustle of a clamorous glittering hall, next in a whispering underworld where trains and travellers loitered and from which return was forbidden. For he saw a native American who, consulting the oracles, on the instant took to his heels and fled up the one descending staircase. By truly prodigious effort, he won his way almost to street level. But there,

18

bracing himself for a final leap, he put down his suitcase. It was enough. And George, conforming to the custom of the country, left him lying in the dust.

777, the Dakota train, a steam locomotive, four coaches and a baggage car, turned out to be one of those extraordinary contraptions which Americans abroad either keep quiet about or hint may survive only on Wild Western film lots. Each car was furnished with high-back couches in button-quilted faded red plush, a baroque cast-iron coal stove and its ancillaries, a fire-extinguisher and a longhandled feather duster. There also was an ominous rack of snow flares, two axes and a massive crowbar.

It all had a Terminus Vladivostok look about it and, to flesh this fancy, the train's conductor, a sad-looking man, began calling out its destination, 'RAPID CITY . . . RAPID CITY . . .' with a desperate air as though he, for one, had no great belief in an arrival there. (And this was by no means unlikely for the steel tracks – but not the tie-rods – had been purchased in 1911 from the Trans-Siberian Railway which, supposing that its useful life was over, had torn it up.)

George checked his case into the baggage car, arranged his cavalry mackintosh and umbrella on the rack and chose a seat by a window through which it seemed likely the sun would shine when they emerged into daylit America. He no longer was buoyed by that exciting optimism with which he had set out almost a week earlier and, later, confessed that, had he possessed the fare, he would have turned tail then and there. 'You see,' he explained, 'all at once the immensity of North America quite overwhelmed me.

19

But yet, in it, not a single soul cared whether I lived or died.'

In this distressingly low state he spread his large hands across his waistcoat, leaned back and shut his eyes on the prospect before him. In vain. The conductor was calling their proposed itinerary, a ribbon of unlikely names unwinding itself westwards across the plains – Ocobomowroc . . . Kendall's Dam . . . Hustler . . . Sparta . . . La Crosse . . . (dusk on the Mississippi) . . . Eyota . . . Owatonna . . . Waseca . . . Smith's Mill . . . (nightfall) . . . Mankato . . . New Ulm . . . Sleepy Eye . . . Essig . . . Revere . . . Walnut Grove . . . (the dog-watches) . . . Tracy . . . Currant Lake . . . Ivanhow . . . Florence . . . Verdi . . . Pipestone . . . Flandreau . . . Lone Tree . . . (across the shifting Missouri) . . . Fort Pierre . . . Whiteclay Butte . . . (another morning, another afternoon) . . . Grindstone . . . Muddy Creek . . .

George's courage flagged.

The true reason for his journey can now be revealed. Like numerous Englishmen, early in life he had been trapped into a deep infatuation with the Wild West by such compelling evangelists as W. B. Hart, Hoot Gibson, Hopalong Cassidy. But whereas with the jamming of a last cap-firing six-shooter most of us break faith with that dreamland, he had turned to grubbing up biographical details of its dead heroes. And these he hoped to collect into a publishable book, Gidner's *Brief Lives of the Frontier*. No one knew of this for he sensed that such an activity might seem pretentious, even suspicious. But secretly he felt rather smug about this self-awarded literary aura and, because the labour split itself into nice little episodes each sustaining a life of its own, the book had not dragged itself off to die in some bottom drawer.

So now, to combat despair, he took his Waterman fountain pen (a parting gift from Balaclava Road Elementary) and the dog-eared file and began working up Brief Life No. 67, 'Joseph Smith, d. 1869, known also as Preacher Smith, Martyr Smith', whose life had been brief indeed, having been abruptly ended by an Oglala Sioux war-party as, tardily and alone, he tracked after the flock which had strayed from his mission church – a gold strike having been announced in Deadwood Gulch.

He was toying with the relative merits of 'He nailed on his tabernackle door the message, GONE TO DEAD-WOOD GOD WILLING' and 'CALLED BY GOD TO DEAD-WOOD', when, glancing up, he saw a ravishingly lovely young woman entering the coach. A wide-brimmed straw hat was perched on her platinum-blonde hair; she was wearing a crimson silk dustcoat. Swaying forward, she spread her sleek self on a couch across the gangway and flashed big bursts of gorgeousness.

Drab, doomstruck Preacher Smith was no match for this vision of delight and George stared hungrily. Just then the train shuddered, hesitantly dragging itself from the underworld, and this exciting creature turned a green and lively eye on him, calling with dauntless confidence, 'Hi there! Say, this is going to be an awful long trip. Let's get acquainted right now. You are a European: this I figure from your outfit.' And with an easy wriggle and swirl, she rearranged herself beside him. 'It's your natty tweed,' she said, 'and that I simply must touch,' running a scarlet nail up and behind his lapel, so that he felt stroked down to the skin. And it being a warm afternoon and the coach swaying gently, he felt rather excitingly uncomfortable.

Why elaborate? Let it be enough that he immediately fell in love and the United States happily resumed that same tingling promise offered months before by Bartholomew's World Atlas. So, lulled in a silky-thighed and heady-perfumed euphoria, he knew with utter certainty that he was crossing the threshold of a marvellous new life. At reasonable intervals, he would sire a succession of healthy, handsome Anglo-Americans and, this splendid creature by his side, would watch the boys become what their class year-books would describe as Outstanding Citizens, whilst the little girls bloomed into Packages of All-round Loveliness or, at the very minimum, Great Home-makers. Of course he didn't yet know these American benedictions but was thinking their Yorkshire equivalents.

So, proprietorially he admired the tiny mole on a nearer cheek; it gave emphasis to her peach-bloom colouring. And he confided to her his prediction that his American Year would make him a Different Man (but had not supposed this change would come so soon or so dramatically). And she confided that America's true wealth was the industry, know-how and integrity of the American people, that, from coast to coast, American food was same as it was safe, that there were 87 identifiable flavours of American ice-cream, that American women could choose from 163 shoe-sizes and that a new magazine dedicated to literary digestion had made it needless ever again to read a book. She also murmured that she favoured tall, strong, blue-eyed men upstanding in good-quality footwear and with a positive attitude towards religion and hard work.

And when, during a leg-stretching intermission at New Lisbon, Wisconsin, he saw that she was sturdier than he had supposed, she perceptively remarked, 'You're dead right, George; I've long years of hard wear left.' So they strolled off and, in the depot's deep shadow, grabbed each other and kissed long and passionately. During this encounter he demonstrated a pressing need for her but thought it premature to put this into words.

Then, when the conductor had recalled the passengers, his fiancée (for all intent and purpose) told him that she must away to the Women's Exclusive where, fending off babies doing more gooey things than a fertilizer-spreader, she must camp that night. And leaving him nodding stupidly, she was gone.

'But darling . . .' Disconcertingly she was back, a long painted nail stabbing at Preacher Smith, 'but darling, in these United States there is no "k" in "tabernacle". I tell you this only because us American taxpayers are just crazy for our kids to spell real good.'

Night fell on Minnesota. Its whistle wailing, 777 bounded across Winona's Mississippi Bridge; the town lights flared and were gone. With his future bride abed, America's blaze too had shrunk to a dull glow and, once more, George turned on poor Smith. But now, breathing life into that long mouldered

23

cadaver had become no more than a drab exercise. He had met his first American woman. Might not the sub-continent be brimful with similarly heady creatures? Had he perhaps been too precipitate in staking so early a claim? Should he not have awaited what Palisades itself might have to offer?

Then it was midnight. But neither a starry nor silent one. Each halt was a ceremony as bands of teenagers welcomed missionary teachers from Back East into the enveloping blackness. EYOTA . . . OWATONNA . . . WASECA . . . TOLSTOI . . . VLADI-VOSTOK . . . each fitfully lit name reminding him that he was plunging deeper into a wildly foreign land. He gritted his teeth and hung on to Preacher Smith. 'But on the trail, with no succour save the Word of God, he fell amongst Oglala Sioux who shamefully stripped him of his raiment and beat out his brains . . .' 'Stripped him of his raiment . . .' the phrase had a naggingly familiar ring. ROME . . . SLEEPY EYE . . . SUGAR BUSH . . . tolling a warning at remote crossings to hidden farms, desolately wailing an approach to sleeping towns, they shuffled westward. Again his spirits sagged.

A neighbour sank flat, spread the *Milwaukee Forum-Herald* across his face and groaned off to sleep. Down the coach, three poker-players huddled beneath a brighter lamp; the top-coated brakeman watched impassively. The roof lights turned blue, the card school folded, stuffed tickets into their hatbands and composed themselves to slumber. And George too, bundling his jacket and mackintosh into a pillow, fell asleep, awakening only once to be momentarily charmed by a busy little steamer puffing across a brilliantly lit lake, a scene of quite theatrical gaiety. Years later, he often recalled this sight but, when he looked up maps of the region, no lake lay athwart their route. And yet he almost could have touched the boat's deck.

Unknown to him, GREYBIRD . . . KIEV . . . METTER-NICH . . . BELCHER'S FORD . . . moved forward to slip back into the night. Stealthily checking hatbands, the conductor shook awake the diminishing company and, one by one, distributed them along the trail. The stars faded, the seemingly endless plains turned grey . . . FEATHER . . . MIGGSVILLE . . . LAST GOOD-BYE . . . DE SMET . . . At HURON the last American left the coach.

Two hours later, he was shaken awake. And, as from a cloud, a voice, the conductor's voice who, justifying his family reputation as a rare wag, was grating out his parody of the revivalist hymn, 'Beulah Land',

'We've reached a land of dust and stones
Where nothing grows but buffalo bones . . .'

Struggling to his feet, swaying with the train, George stared unbelievingly at the science-fiction landscape which had crept upon him in the night . . . stricken trees, boarded-up, tar-paper-patched farmhouses, collapsing barns, all pitching around a vast sea of bleached grass and dying corn which heaved off to the rim of a pitiless sky. It recalled a childhood memory of a grocer's calendar decorating his parents' outside privy, 'After Trafalgar', a pictorial disaster littered with shattered spars, listing hulks and drowning mariners.

A red meccano bridge spanned a near-dry river, a mob of cattle shouldered a windpump above an exhausted waterhole and, away on the further bluffs,

25

like a beached sea-monster, some sort of store. A store with a flagpole. And a man! A man shading his eyes against the brilliant sky quivering with heat, watching the train pass. Why, there's a man out there, he thought. People live here.

The conductor dumped his suitcase on the seat and glanced curiously at him. 'Your baggage,' he said. 'Welcome to Dakota, the Sunshine State.'

George pulled himself together. 'The young lady . . .' he muttered. 'That young woman . . . you may have noticed us together last night. Well, early this morning I suppose. We took a stroll along the platform at New Lisbon. She slept in the Women's Exclusive.'

'Big girl, good-looker? Sure, I remember her. Left the train in Minnesota. Sleepy-Eye . . . no, Crystal Lake. Four hours back. Nope, left no message.'

'No? Oh!'

'Could be she forgot.'

'Yes, I suppose so.'

'She visited with you. But you were hard on. Lingered a spell looking down at you. Dewy eyed. Then she remarked, "Conductor, when he makes Dakota, see he don't forget the gamp and mackintosh. He's a Rainmaker and they surely need him out there." Kinda joke, see?'

777 braked. A scatter of frame houses, a water tower, then a huddle of warehouses, then the roundhouse, then the depot. 'Palisades!' the conductor cried down the empty coach. 'This is Palisades. Palisades, s. d.'

*   *   *

'No, of course they shouldn't have let me go. With hindsight, any fathead can see that. But that pair at the Goodwill League knew no more about you Americans than I did. Like me, I suppose they'd never even seen one.

'Nobody told me that yours was a wildly foreign shore.

'Why are you laughing?'

Mr Gidner prodded the fire: it glowered back at him.

'That I LOVE LUCY *on your T-shirt?' he grumbled. 'Who's Lucy?'*

Henry Farewell and Mr Ardvaak were seated on the shaded staging which fronted the store at Pollocks Crossing and rocked gently in their chairs. Before them a gravel road plunged steeply to the river, reared up the Bitter-root's bluffs and turned south along a line of posts and sagging wires marking the railroad's track to Palisades.

The blind storekeeper was wearing a faded blue collarless shirt and coarse canvas dungarees but, despite the early morning heat, the banker, buttoned up in his pepper and salt suit, might have been awaiting a valued depositor. He was gazing mildly towards the far-off farmhouses and barns ruffling the grassland washing around them: at this time of day and in the evenings he found the prairie's sameness most agreeable.

'Life slips away, James,' he said, 'yet little enough to show for it. Here, in Teddy County . . .'

He was silent, seeming to have lost the drift of his argument.

'Here we live in this drab little settlement . . .'

He stopped again.

'Yet most of us never leave it, jockey for its insignificant honours, tidy it, loot it, glare with a jaundiced eye at the world beyond it, become hysterical at a possibility of being buried outside it. And why? Why? Nothing changes. Each year has inexorable sameness. The School Year begins, then Thanksgiving gluttony, then Christmas hysteria, the Basketball Tourney, the black winter intermission . . . well, this you know. I try to live hopefully, yet but for my little library, my Fielding, Trollope, poor Sterne, there are times when I believe I might hang myself.'

'Suits me fine,' replied Mr Ardvaak, 'but get your drift.'

'I fancy that our great Longfellow felt similarly,' the banker went on,

> 'Tell me not in mournful numbers
> Life is but an empty dream.

Ah, but what are we to make of his next but one line?

> And things are not what they seem.

Now there's a thought. (And, for Longfellow, a deep one.)'

He stood up, stepping from the porch's deep shadow and looked north along the river bluffs. '777 is almost due,' he said. 'It has been a day and a night on its way. Is this why its passing excites one, James? We ask, "Bringing What? Bringing Whom? Perhaps bringing nothing but a reminder that 'things are not what they seem'?"'

He shaded his eyes against the sun's glare to watch

the train. And, unknowing, that is how George Gidner first saw him.

The locomotive came to a panting halt; the town yawned before the traveller. There was no cosy refreshment-room, hissing tea-urn, Ladies Waiting Room, W. H. Smith bookstall, all these sheltering comfortably beneath a filthy glass canopy supported by ornamental cast-iron pillars – that borderland arranged by the British for the collection of luggage and composure. This emphatically was PALISADES, U.S.A. where people only got on or got off, whilst 777 gasped impatiently athwart Oxbow, its main street (planned wide enough to swing a wagon and team). Immediately, uncompromisingly and (to George Gidner) threateningly, was a prospect of false-fronted buildings, peeling paint, a mad muddle of power lines, a blank and brutal sky. This irreversibly was It.

Gathering his few possessions, he teetered on the blisteringly hot brink. Then over it.

Now, at long last, he stood upon ground hallowed by bloody footfalls treading the pages of his *Brief Lives*. But there was no surge of excitement. Rather, he ruefully recognized his change of circumstance. On the train he had been a tourist, no more than a mildly alarmed spectator of the parched plains and dying farms. Back in his book, he could have drawn the reader's attention to the awfulness of Oxbow Avenue, patronizingly hinted at the aching tedium of a lifetime in Palisades, then rolled heedlessly onward. But now he was a horrified participant. Bradford's Municipal Tramways, the Lancashire & Yorkshire Railway Company, the White Star Line, the Chicago &

Northwestern Railroad, all these had fulfilled their contracts to drop him spot on the name he once had exulted over. He had become a new feature of that name and a layabout sprawling on the ticket-office step shot a confirmatory ball of tobacco juice at his beautifully polished veldtshoen.

So, burdened by suitcase, mackintosh and umbrella, clamped into his tweed suit, he doggedly made his way through the dust towards the highway where a band of citizens, uttering shrill cries of welcome, had cascaded upon a returning native. It would have been cheering to report that one Palisadan, espying George's foreignness, detached himself from the joyful throng and held out a warm hand of welcome to the plains. Sadly, no. And worse, his sole acquaintance in North America was about to forsake him: the conductor was calling a last summons to the Black Hills.

'HOLLOBIRD . . . MISSOURI BRIDGE . . . PIERRE . . . FORT PIERRE . . . BATTLE CREEK . . . OTUMNA . . . PLUM'S BUTTE . . .' He remounted the steps of the leading coach, looked down on his late passenger and raised his eyebrows. A last invitation to flight? George Gidner's spirit quailed, his body sagged, the lovely American's perfidy caught at his heart.

He stood his ground.

The peevish clerk back at the Anglo-American Goodwill League would have been proud of him.

QUINN . . . WALL . . . BOXELDER . . . the loco's bell jangled, empty coaches jerked and, plummetting steam and smoke, 777 shuffled off westward . . . RAPID CITY (debouch for DEADWOOD) . . . IRON CREEK (change for LEAD) . . . HOTSPRINGS . . . CUSTER . . .

ROCKERVILLE . . . SPEARFISH (change for HOMESTAKE GOLD MINES) . . . TERMINUS FALLS. George watched it puff out of his life: it had been a sort of home.

Beyond the now empty track a drunk was lying, snugly wrapped in the stink of last night's booze, coat shuffled up back, head cradled in arms. A police car wailed. Two deadfaced cops dawdled across to the slumberer, levered him over with their boots and, taking a foot apiece, battered his soles with their heavy night-sticks. The citizen moaned, stirred, pulled his knees to his chin: the beating did not abate. Without turning to identify his attackers, he tottered up and shambled away to collapse in some safer ditch.

The Welcome Home party had watched with eager interest. One cried joyfully, 'Police-Chief Gorkev's launched his re-election drive early this year.' They hooted.

The cops strode manfully back to their vehicle, slammed doors, gunned the engine, sped. This brief scene of savagery made a deep impression upon George, and, long afterwards, he remarked, 'You know, I don't expect to be believed, but the morning turned colder. As if not just the sun but America had turned its darker side towards me (if you follow what I mean, though I don't suppose you do). And, later of course, at Pollocks Crossing, I felt the same. Though what was done there, was done in the darkness. Yes, in the dark. Naturally!'

He trudged off up Oxbow, passing what he later learned were the town's principal architectural monuments – the Roundhouse, Vogler's Saloon and Cigar Store (the hellers' hangout), Teddy County Courthouse, the Rialto Movie Theater, the offices of *The*

31

Prairie Plow newspaper, Farewell's Dime & Nickel Store (which a blonde giantess in an overtight skirt was languidly opening up for business). And then, solid granite, safe as a rock, THE BITTER-ROOT VALLEY SETTLERS' BANK, FOUNDED 1881. He checked its proclamation against the address on an envelope and, dragging back its inner doors, crossed the threshold to transact his first financial negotiation in North America.

Three counters were arranged around a marble floor on which were sited a drinking fountain, a small catafalque, and several chrome-plated machines dispensing gob-stoppers. Below a sign,

THE BUSINESS OF AMERICA IS BUSINESS.
YOUR BUSINESS IS OUR SACRED TRUST.

and behind a steel grille, he glimpsed the powerful brass engines of a safe and, as he stood hesitantly, taking in all this, two tellers and three young lady cashiers looked speculatively at him. Plainly he was from a distant, damper and colder clime. Maine? Perhaps even Canada?

And Henry B. Farewell (The first, *Fare*, was the emphatic syllable), the Bank's president – with total executive authority – just in from an early morning jaunt to Pollocks Crossing, swayed gently in his rocking chair and smiled. A brief letter from Bradford Education Committee, enclosing a meagre cheque, had heralded a new customer's coming and his splendidly protective garments announced that he had come. So, nervously running a forefinger along his untidy moustache (concealing a hint of a harelip) and stirring his small hands as if making ineffectual strokes to save himself from drowning, he stepped forward.

'Ah, Mr Gidner!' he exclaimed in an unusually light voice. 'It *is* Mr Gidner? Mr George G. Gidner? Yes? Then welcome to my bank, sir. You find it unfamiliar? Even bizarre? This I can understand. Ah, but already you must have observed that, in these United States, money is not the secret thing it is with you. No? Well, such is an impression from my reading. A doubtlessly imperfect one: after all, I am no more than a bird of passage winging across the pages of your great literature. You must forgive my carpet-slippers; I was up and about early and the heat . . . well, my feet swell.' All this came breathlessly, hesitantly, anxiously. And with a faintly stagey sound.

Then he smiled and added, 'But sir, I am neglecting your business which, as you will have observed, is our Sacred Trust. I am happy to tell you that a month's salary has preceded you.' And, motioning to a cashier, he handed over the seventy-eight dollars which were to sustain George for a calendar month. Then, seeking an address for the bank's records, he was told that his new client had none, that he knew no more of the town than could be picked up on a plod from the railway station but that now, with local currency in his pocket, he would begin seeking digs, preferably a bed-sitter which he hoped would not knock him back more than twenty-six bob a week, inclusive of washing, some mending and darning, a cooked breakfast, lunch, plain tea and maybe a mug of cocoa and a bite last thing (but not toasted cheese as this brought on alarming delusions that he was dead).

' "Twenty-six bob",' Henry Farewell murmured,

33

savouring this uncompromisingly impossible catalogue of desire, ' "and a mug of cocoa last thing".'
(And why had he never heard of this hallucinatory
property of toasted cheese? Neither Samuel Richardson nor Laurence Sterne, not even the encyclopaedic
Trollope had anywhere referred to the phenomenon.
Perhaps a particular brand of cheese? Cheddar?
Stilton? Ah, Double Gloucester! This last sounded
formidable enough to fit the ticket. And, at the same
time, he stifled a wish to learn the difference between
'Tea' and 'Tea-with-Hovis' to which, only last evening, P. G. Wodehouse had drawn his attention. The
novel's hero had consumed such a meal in a windy
back-garden in the Cotswold Hills whilst pursuing a
prize pig and had been charged half-a-crown.) But he
did not voice these speculations. Instead he lamented,
' "A bite-last-thing", a "bed-sitter", "digs" . . . alas
sir, I fear you will discover none of these desirable
institutions in Palisades. Perhaps not anywhere in
these United States. Here, if you are not a house-
holder, you must rent a room and eat out.'

'Eat out!' George exclaimed. 'Good gracious!
Where?'

'In cafés and lunch-bars. Where else? A rented
room will cost you twelve dollars a month. A room
with closet, fourteen dollars. Thus, you will have a
balance of sixty-four dollars with which to buy three
meals a day for thirty days. Alas, even with a
discounted punch-hole card . . .' He shook his head
sympathetically at hard times ahead. 'Then there are
those other sovereign necessities for survival on our
northern plains. For instance – your wardrobe! Our
winters are of notable savagery.'

34

Although too ignorant of commodity prices to plumb the precise depth of impending pauperism, George Gidner quailed at the prospect before him. And his new aquaintance happily read his mind.

'For a trifling five dollars a month I can rent you a room with closet at my residence,' he said. 'A spacious room, a far, far better room than I myself occupy. This splendid room fronts Oxbow where from a comfortable chair (which I shall transfer from a less-favoured tenant's room) may be observed the ebb and flow of Palisadan and therefore (in miniature) American life. Also, at special rates, I can arrange for Mrs Georgina Lahnstein to launder for you; let us say fifteen cents per shirt, five cents each detachable collar, one cent a sock or handkerchief. (You could cleanse soiled nether garments free of charge whilst taking a shower.) And, as an introductory offer, I should waive your first month's rent. Or let us say, as a gesture to international brotherhood.'

'Thank you,' George said. 'This is frightfully generous of you; in fact, you've saved my bacon and I am greatly obliged to you, Mr Farewell. And I agree to your terms.'

'In the evening the two of us will talk about England. Occasionally, of Wales and Scotland. But not Ireland I think . . . But particularly of your eighteenth-century authors by whom I am much taken, so much so that a Yale professor who passed this way diagnosed strong traces of their vocabulary in my own conversational style. Perhaps you already have observed this? (Smollett, Fielding and such.) And perhaps we might approach our own times and discuss Trollope, Kipling and, of course, G. A. Henty.

Now, how would you assess their separate merits as chroniclers of Empire? Well, another time perhaps . . . And certain institutions puzzle me. May I cite examples? The inns which figure so much in Fielding's *Tom Jones* – the barmaids who succeeded the earlier tapsters; what precisely were their duties? Was more expected of them than drawing beer? And, if so, how much more?'

Then observing his new tenant's face to fall at this elaboration of his lease, he added swiftly, 'And, naturally, in return I shall interpret America, draw your attention to delicate nuances of our national persona which might otherwise escape your attention. For why else but to observe us can you have come so far to live in our insignificant community? Although you have come to teach, there is much to learn. Ah, do not be deceived that, because we share the English tongue, we are not so foreign as the Chinese. We are not to be relied upon. Turn up the American sack and strange, alarming, even dangerous things may come tumbling out. Alas, yes. Ah, here is my motherless daughter.

'Becky, honey,' he said, 'this is Mr Gidner who has come to join your High School faculty. He will be rooming with us.'

'I need to have twenty bucks,' the girl said sourly. 'The ball-game at Huron. And for godsake don't wait up for me. That old witch, Turton, neither.' She took the bills before glancing balefully at George. 'Hi!' she hissed. And went.

Then, for a moment or two, neither spoke. Yet each regarded the other with utmost attention. George Gidner, because the banker was the intermediary through which he would receive his monthly dollar dole and whose rooftree must be his refuge. Henry Farewell, because he had decided that this young man who, unpredictably, had exiled himself, should help while away tedious winter evenings in pleasant speculation on his own literary wanderings, interpret half-understood encounters with those other Englishmen thronging the magnificently bound volumes on the shelves in his cosy study. 'Twenty-six bob', 'bedsitter', he thought happily. What a splendidly promising beginning!

Or so both believed.

But uneasily, each, in his bones, knew that their meeting had an unexplained significance. And years later George Gidner told a confidant, 'Don't run away with the notion that our coming together from the ends of the earth (as dear old Kipling would have put it) had been arranged in Fate's dark womb. (Unless, of course, Fate is an uneasy feeling in the pit of one's stomach that something is happening which one doesn't want to happen but can't stop happening.) All the same (and I'll never forget this), when I reached the bank door, I simply had to turn. Had to! No other way of putting it. And there he stood. Stock still! Exactly as I'd left him. Hadn't stirred an inch. Staring at me as I was at him. And, by Jove, until that minute, I hadn't cottoned on to how lanky a chap he was. Nor how unnaturally small were his extremities – hands, feet, even his head. There he was, one ankle wound round the other. And do you know what entered my head – like a flash: He's like a big bird that's forgotten how to fly. Odd wasn't it?

'And I knew that he, too, felt that something . . .

well, something queer had happened and yet couldn't put a finger on what it was. For the both of us I suppose you could say that the weeks and months ahead were being flicked over like pages in a book but too fast for reading: yet had we learnt the trick of it, might have seen how it all would end. And, that known, I suppose I would have hoofed it back to the railroad depot and bought a ticket as far back east as seventy-eight dollars would carry me.'

The Homesteader Hotel (thirty-six rooms numbered 100 to 360) towered four and a half floors above the intersection of Oxbow and 2nd Street. Its basement was a pool-room where mildly desperate men knocked balls about and used bad language; its ground floor offered Reception and the Kwikbite Coffee Shop. And, blundering into this cave and near to terminal dehydration, George mounted a tall stool and called for a drink.

Mr Aristotle Stavros, its swarthy concessionary, put before him what he believed might have been ordered and, because this was the first stranger he had seen for several weeks, watched him with a lively curiosity. He then considered it commercially safe to observe that his customer seemed to be in a distressed condition.

'It is this intense heat,' George explained. 'At present, it is a trifle too much for me. Given time, of course, I shall adjust. However, since you have mentioned it, yes, I must confess that I am rather overcome.' And, warmed by Mr Stavros's interest and sympathy, he explained what had brought him to Palisades, feelingly described the long journey (though omitting the tale of his beautiful betrayer) and his great satisfaction at arranging accommodation so speedily.

'Mr Henry Farewell is one of our finest citizens; he has a great heart,' Mr Stavros thought it safe to state, adding that he could be quoted upon this. 'He also plays very elegantly upon the bassoon. Yet is he no addlepate. No sir! Fifteen banks east of the River have gone bust but not our Bitter-root Valley Bank. Mr Farewell's bank, sir, is as safe as the Homestake Gold Mine (and you may quote me upon that also).' He then tapped his brow which George took to be an ultimate confirmation of his landlord's commercial sagacity.

'Now me,' Mr Stavros went on but in lower tones, 'now me, as you will have observed, am a Greek. (You will appreciate that we are now in session.) I personally have not visited Greece but I am a Greek and can thus sympathize with the distress of another European in this godawful climate. (You may not quote me.)'

He then earnestly counselled George to eat and drink slow, in fact, to do everything slow except think. 'Do not let the Americans straight-arm you into an early grave, Mr Gidner. (For graves do not come cheap in this country.) Every last American scares if nothing goes. They learn at their mothers' breasts that they must be up and doing each waking hour God gives them. And this is the Big Killer. I shall pause now whilst you glance casually over your left shoulder at that man yonder, as he illustrates my message to a T. (And now we are very much in session.)'

One of the policemen who had attacked the railroad drunk was slumped across the bar talking to himself around a half-eaten cigar. 'That gorilla is Police-Chief Gorkev and he is one big hoodlum and chiseller from Illinois. It is not enough for him to keep traffic moving and our neighbourhood safe for little children and nice old ladies. No sir, I have heard tell that he has gotten himself a mail-order Thomson sub-machine gun, dreams himself back in Chicago and chases around town seeking agitators, liberals and bleeding-hearts. Which are hard to come upon in Palisades. Do not be any of those things, my friend, because you would not appreciate a session without witnesses in the society of Police-Chief Gorkev.

'Mercifully his days are numbered and I have laid a small wager with my wife's sister's husband that he will be parcelled up well ahead of next but one Thanksgiving.' And, as the soon sorely-to-be-missed monster dug his spoon deep into a strawberry impreg-nated ice-cream, causing it to ooze into chocolate sauce and reveal a succulent core of banana, he added triumphantly, 'See what I mean? Stepping on the gas! My, some funeral-parlour beautician is going to roll real hard to have that ape grin back at the mourners.'

'Funeral parlour'! This chilling combination of death and Sunday tea with an aunt, albeit imperfectly understood, was enough to make George do a couple of relaxing knee-bends and draw several deep breaths.

'I shall let nothing agitate me,' he promised. 'Nothing!' And when Mr Stavros asked for this to be repeated, he knew how well he was observing this new friend's counsel – he already was speaking in whispers.

The bartender then asked if he would like to view the town with a very minimum of exertion and led him to a venerable elevator. It groaned upwards to the mezzanine floor and paused whilst, with proper pride, his attention was drawn to the twilit chamber where the Rotary Club, Kiwanis Club, Lions' Club and the Knights of Columbus ate lunch and heard speeches. Then they rose to a last base-camp from which they struck out on foot, then up a ladder and through a skylight to the Homesteader's roof.

Peering gingerly over its parapet, George saw that the town was a grid of six streets crossed by six avenues, each sidewalk verge thickly planted with cottonwoods and chinese elms. It is not a Real Town like Bradford, he thought. It is a small forest with houses in it. Then, gazing further afield, he saw that this inhabited woodland was planted on an immense carpet of farmland, its monotonous pattern of one-mile squares bounded by dirt roads and green tracks and punctuated by dying windbreaks. From skyline to skyline, the sluggish Bitter-root crawled between its bluffs; a railroad track rushing arrow-straight east and west cut across another rushing arrow-straight south to north. And, upon this crushing sameness, Palisades diminished into no more than a crossroads which had bulged a little more when a family felt that it had ventured far enough westwards or had been thrust back from the plains by poverty, disease or old age. Great heaven! he thought, it is a sort of desert. It *is* a desert.

'Do not be alarmed,' Mr Stavros murmured. 'Us Europeans need never go out there. Nothing beyond our city limits need ever concern us. And what you cannot see, because it lies beyond what you can see, is just the same. Mitchell – it is Palisades with a Corn Palace. Huron – Palisades with the State Fairground. And Aberdeen, Watertown, Brookings – all just the same. Samesville, Samesburg, Same City, Fort Same! Wyoming also. And Nebraska. Kansas also, I have heard said. Some higher, some flatter, some windier, some hotter. But the same. Just the same.'

'But are there not people, Americans, out there?' George asked.

'You are real smart,' Mr Stavros cried admiringly. 'It is inhabited. And on Saturdays they come to town. With your own eyes you will see them. Ha! And because we are strictly in session, I can tell you that they are tightwads. Also savages. Reliable statistics reveal that in this State, 3,847 of their dwellings have no interior privy.' He announced this with great passion, a sweat of hate starting from his brow. But then, recalling his own advice he let his arms flop limply to his sides and forced a ghastly smile. 'But Athens, Mr Gidner, you should visit Athens, Greece. That is some city.' And was himself again.

George knitted his forehead at the prospect before and below him. He recalled the desertion in the darkness, the spit-wad shooter at the depot, the strangeness of Henry B. Farewell, the brutish Police-Chief who, to fulfil a prophecy, must drop dead before some Thanksgiving-for-he-knew-not-what. And now, this new and awful manifestation of America.

They descended in silence. Before parting Mr Stavros gave George a handful of match-booklets boosting his brother-in-law's Parthenon All-Nite Diner. Then shepherding him to the edge of the fiery

42

sidewalk, he pointed the direction of the Farewell Rooming House. His last words were not to hurry there.

Next day, the combined faculties of the town's schools were herded into the Senior High gymnasium to be pepped up by a peripatetic educator from Back East for the long year ahead.

'Forget you are a teacher, a boring person, a sadsack, a grind,' this missionary cried. 'From this day henceforth *you* can be a life-enhancer, a Mr (or Miss) Wonderful.' These encouraging words stirred George and, paying unwitting tribute to American salesmen (the flower of the nation), he leaned from the forward edge of his hard seat, happy that the process of becoming Another Person was getting under way.

'Personality enrichment', 'Intellectual re-tooling', 'Accultural acquisition' – these splendid rallying cries banged about the climbing bars and echoed in his heart. Until he glanced around.

His fellow workers either stared impassively at the evangelist, studied an unusually plain ceiling or, having orientated their faces towards the source of sound from the podium, had closed their eyes and minds against possibility of metamorphosis. Plainly no one saw him/herself as Mr/Mrs/Miss Wonderful. The year ahead was going to be the all too familiar blistering drag at the oars, many would be the vicissitudes suffered, small the dollar reward.

George Gidner weighed words against faces. He profitably recalled Mr Stavros's warning not to become a funeral charge on his parents and, taking deep breaths to lower his pulse rate, slouched back on his seat, let the Burning Message wing over him to the blue beyond. Then, finding it difficult to maintain a blank mind, he fretted uneasily over his inadequate answers to his landlord's yesterday's inquisition on British pubs, guest-houses and hotels and their relative sanitary arrangements.

After a long while there was some polite applause and the educator slipped off to catch his train. The Superintendent of Schools then announced seven new recruits to the Palisades Schools System. 'On hearing your name,' he called, 'you will rise and be recognized.' Bodies stirred, eyes brightened. 'So this bilious sourpuss must be suffered next door up the hall for a twelvemonth?' 'Might not this dewy-eyed creature have a thing going for a balding grade-school principal with nicotined dentures and four married daughters?' And, properly, George's foreignness rated close attention for, in those far-off days, Europe was many days distant and only veterans of the 1917 Expeditionary Force had set eyes upon an Englishman. So he was examined with unusual interest, his weight and height calculated, the unsuitability of his clothing marvelled at, his love-quotient assessed, the unjustly high salary with which the School Board had lured him from his green and pleasant island bitterly censured.

'I shall depart from custom and call upon George G. Gidner to say something,' the Superintendent announced – doubtlessly to reassure his subordinates that they were not to be burdened with a language problem. No public institution ever before had invited George to address it, but he managed to mutter his delight at finding himself in Palisades and that he was enjoying the unusually settled weather. This

44

drew mild applause and a man in the next seat shook his hand warmly, saying, 'Hadtlestadt (Speech and Debate) – say, that was some declam. My old Grandpa was an Englishman from the city of Norfolk and, because of this, I could follow every word you uttered. Am not so aged as you may be supposing. Thirty-two in fact, no more than. My hair I lost being required unjustly to sponsor the Junior Prom four years in a row. Have much hope it will come again: my wife don't like me this way.'

The Superintendent then drew a harrowing picture of a superintendent clinging to a diminishing tax-base and menaced by snarling ratepayers, before acquainting his hearers with news that, without dissent, the School Board had voted a round-the-table five per cent pay-cut, that henceforward no house-owning teacher might dwell beyond the city's tax limits, that voluntary unpaid chores had become compulsory unpaid chores, that male teachers must continue to smoke only in the boiler-room and female teachers not at all, that unless a teacher heard that he/she was re-hired at the close of the school year, he/she must assume him/herself fired.

There was some uneasy stirring at this ukase: it died when attention was drawn to a School Board vote of 5 to 0 against giving Miss Leila Nulty (American Literature, Soft-ball and Stenography) a hearing against her dismissal for clinch-foxtrotting with one of her students in the dimly lit backroom of the Parthenon Café.

In conclusion he read a cyclostyled message from the State Governor urging unremitting vigilance against recidivists hostile to the American Way of

45

Life. And the session was finalized by an appeal that, after putting a dime in the tinkle-dish, teachers should intermingle and communicate socially. Sanka coffee and low calorie doughnuts would be served.

High School Principal Moskvin wore rimless hexagonal eyeglasses, had a deadstraight centre-parting and a phonographic voice. He sat like a ramrod in his chair and, but for a tinted studio portrait of his mother and father, his desk top was bare. On the wall behind him George Washington was crossing the ice-strewn Delaware to close with the British.

'Ah, our Englishman!' he said. And repeated this only a little less sourly. 'You must be processed by our Behavioural Acceptability Battery. Unless you harbour anti-social traits or dotalistic deviationary trends, you need fear nothing.'

He did not smile whilst making this pronouncement and then handed George a sheaf of questions, each succeeded by AFFIRMATIVE/NEGATIVE/UNAPPREHENDED:

1. Are you troubled by thoughts of heaven and hell?
2. Is your sleep fitful?
3. Do you believe that everything in the Holy Bible is turning out as the prophets foretold?
4. Do you believe the American ethic to be an upward and ongoing ethic?
5. Is denying the existence of God worse than horsing around during the playing of 'The Star Spangled Banner'?
6. Do you aspire to deeds of deep significance?

46

and so on, AFFIRMATIVE/NEGATIVE/UNAPPRE-
HENDED to 100.

Only the inquiry about deeds of significance gave
George pause. Why else was he working on his *Brief
Lives of the Frontier*? Yet, in an already overcrowded
field of native aspirants, might not such a declaration
by a foreigner be resented? It was one of his two
UNAPPREHENSIONS.

This YES/NO/DON'T KNOW was far the most pleasing feature of American life he had so far met. It was
so much less trying than the English inquisitorial
demand that candidates voice fearless opinions and
then justify them in carefully punctuated prose.
Nevertheless he was put out when Principal Moskvin
did not eagerly pore over his replies to learn what
manner of man he was about to employ but, instead,
told him that the exercise had not been meaningful
because, since he already was here, it was too late to
reject him (though, if the battery exposed him as an
un-American, communistic, psychotic sex-deviate in
failing health, then he might be sure that his contract
would be terminated).

'Now,' he went on, 'a summation of your public
school system as exemplified in *Reader's Digest*
demonstrates that our American and your British
learning philosophies, although divergent, are not
antagonistic. Let us say that they are not one hundred
per cent consistent.' He paused and George, feeling
that a response was expected, timidly assembled the
few American phrases he had picked up and earnestly
asked to be alerted if it was felt that he could locate
effortwise more meaningfully.

To his delight, this was recognized as intelligent

utterance, proof of his worthiness for further instruction.

'Right here, in Grover Cleveland,' Moskvin intoned, 'we operate the Meyerbeer Success Syndrome – A . . . B . . . C . . . D . . . E . . . F. E Passes. F flunks. We here in Grover Cleveland are one hundred per cent anti-flunk. Our students don't go for flunking. The Superintendent don't go for flunking. The School Board don't go for flunking. *I* don't go for flunking. That, in its nutshell, encapsulates our Palisades philosophy. Minor calibrations will be brought to your attention as your performance is monitored and assessed. At all times use dustless chalk.'

He then dismissed George with a chilling smile, a map of the building and an Acceptability Curve which proved that, in Grover Cleveland, there always had been and always must be 20 per cent A-students, 32 per cent B-students, 38 per cent Cs, 6 per cent Ds, 4 per cent Es, and 0 per cent F-students. And with this news he made his way to his assigned home-room which was furnished with desks, wall-blackboards, several sticks of dustless chalk, a large flag in its cast-iron stand and a thick copy of Breitmeyer's *Sentence Diagramming Made Easy*. Above the door was the class motto,

BEYOND LIES THE TIMBER. COME LET US BUILD.

George considered this quite inspiring. But not so inspiring as his own name, GEORGE G. GIDNER, INSTRUCTOR newly painted on the door's glass panel, because this confirmed not only geographically but metaphorically that his long journey was at an end and that Grover Cleveland High and, therefore, the United States of America recognized him.

*   *   *

'You keep asking me why Henry Farewell was so engrossed with English life,' Mr Gidner exclaimed irritably. 'You may as well ask why do folk collect Staffordshire figures or matchbox tops or (for that matter) go to tedious lengths to catalogue the daily doings of Virginia Woolf and her cronies!

'We are here and we fill in time as best we can till comes the dread day. Give it a few more years, my girl, and you will discover that life is a bit of desert.

'You don't follow?

'Well, poor Farewell populated his corner of the wilderness with such company as could be dredged from that little library of his, from Sterne, from Fielding, from half a dozen such. Yes, yes, it was an affectation! And yes, he was a romantic. For all I know you're a romantic. When I was your age I certainly was. Why else do you suppose I went to Dakota?

'Henry Farewell can scarcely have believed his luck when I turned up to be pumped without mercy – grammar schools, dialect, clothes, pubs, parsons . . .

'No, no, I can't explain it. Must there be an explanation?'

He gloomily examined the steel engraving of 'The Death of Nelson' above the fireplace, then rose and carefully straightened his back and then the picture.

A week had passed and, once more, Henry Farewell and his friend, Mr Ardvaak, were seated on the store's porch at Pollocks Crossing.

'Ah, yes indeed (to answer your question, James), I am astonished that I have mentioned before neither Miss Bull nor my long gone English holiday. Come, come! Surely I must have done so? No? Well, it was thus.' (And Henry Farewell rubbed a finger along his moustache.)

'We met by the merest chance. Knowing me as you do (none better) I need not tell you (but I shall) that, although it was my first (and, perhaps last) trip across the Ocean, my resolution was iron: nothing, nothing, would induce me to toil around the European tourist circuit. Nothing!'

Mr Ardvaak shuffled his rocking-chair and turned his face towards the sun.

'So, during the crossing, I studied the purser's gazetteer and selected a small town situate in the middle of the southern part of the island. A bow drawn at a venture! For one of my temperament, impulse is all. Great Minden! The name took my fancy. An eighteenth-century chime, don't you think? No?

'So I caught a train – First Class. (The English do not believe All Men are created Equal.)

'The Fusilier was its sole hotel. Hotel? Inn? And, crossing its threshold, I knew that here was England enough for me. The decision had no basis in reason. Indeed all manifestation denied it. There was no reception desk. Only a bill-of-terms thumb-tacked to a wall. And a bell which I tinkled. And, after a time, the proprietor joined me (Miss Bull, as you will have guessed). Her first, her Christian name, was Isabella.

'Reluctantly she agreed that Yes, it could not be denied that Room 3 was vacant. But, no, it would not suit me. It was without running water and she had heard that Americans cleaned themselves obsessively. In fact, it had no more than a ewer and basin. Though, if against all good sense I stubbornly insisted in staying, no doubt a can of hot shaving water could be left by Annie at my door. At the door! Annie was simple and could not be sure which commercial traveller had been the father of her last child. But would I not be better advised to go on to Oxford? She had been told that several hotels not only had h & c in each room, but the wireless also.

' "Then Number 3 I shall take," I told her. "And for one calendar month. With full board and lodging." What a splendid un-American phrase that is, James! What visions of plenty! It calls to mind the poet, Chesterton,

> To an open house in the evening
> Home shall men come . . .

'And so it was with me. (For it *was* evening and I felt *at home*.) And how well I recall Miss Bull's answer, "You are a chap that makes his mind up a sight too fast. You've not set foot in the room nor tried the bed." (She said this quite sharply.)

'She was right. (As she always was.) For a bed can make or mar a man's contentment. (Can this be denied?) Ah, she was remarkable woman, James. I shall go so far to say that she was the woman I have been looking for all my life. Without knowing it. Until that moment.'

'Expect you hollered, "Marry me Miss Bull",' Mr Ardvaak remarked drily.

'She was married. Although the fellow had sloped off. Where he went I believe she neither knew nor cared. Except for a chance word that he had been a good hand at penmanship and was a walking dictionary, no mention was made of him. I daresay that he

51

found living with her too much for him. (I recall a similar circumstance in Fielding.) So, she had resumed her maiden name and the local magistrates had transferred the inn's licence to it,

ISABELLA BULL
LICENSED TO SELL TOBACCO
& SPIRITUOUS LIQUORS

But that is how she did things. Alternative action was considered, that weighed against this, a decision reached and immediately acted upon. No shilly-shallying! Thus she cleared her mind of those vexations which bear us lesser mortals down.'

The two sat in silence whilst the banker considered the advisability of a next revelation.

'Did she care for me? Yes, I believe that she did; I think that it might be said that she recognized an affinity, some kinship of spirit. I even dare to suppose she may have harboured some small affection for me. Alas, perhaps only for as long as I lived beneath her roof. Well, be that as it may, she dealt fairly with me; any debt is wholly mine.

'Quite often she would say, "I can't make myself love you – if that's what you're hankering after. Heart-whole, that is. For, when all's said and done, what are you but a paying-guest? And a foreigner at that." Nor could she bring herself to call me "Henry". In extravagant moods, she ironically would allude to me as Our Gentleman from the States, as though I was a denizen of some extra-terrestrial world, which she was harbouring because it had knocked on her door.

'Well, to return to our first meeting. I made it immediately clear that I did not propose visits to twenty-one foreign shores in twenty-one days and that, but for a single obligatory night's stay in the north of the country, I should not stir from Great Minden. My aim was to become lost in the local landscape. But how? I consulted Miss Bull. (Well, I shall call her "Bella".) Without hesitation she replied that it was my togs gave the game away, but she knew of a tailor who would fix me up. (As witness the suit I wear only on Occasions. Your seventy-fifth birthday party, James, you will recall.) When I first appeared in it, Miss Bull . . . Bella . . . rubbed the coat's lapel between finger and thumb, remarking to the lad Jonson, "If he can run to this quality cloth, we must suppose that Our Gentleman from the States is a millionaire." At the time, the irony escaped me and I protested that my assets were fluid, flowing in and out like the tide, a true simile because my fled wife and now my difficult daughter spent and spend money like water.'

'Jonson?' Mr Ardvaak murmured.

'Ah yes, Jonson. I am glad Jonson interests you. Doubtlessly he answered to some first name or other, but at The Fusilier he was "Jonson" and his father being the town's principal butcher, he was known to his peers as Kidneys Jonson. He was eighteen and, like the odious Swatt who hangs around my daughter, was a brutish, spot-scourged youth (this last affliction betraying unsatisfied sexual longing, Bella explained). And he complained continually of beatings by savage schoolmasters. (Into whose hands I would deliver Swatt with joy.)

'Frankly, I am satisfied in my mind that he lusted after Miss Bull who was old enough to be . . . almost

53

old enough to be his mother. Certainly he must have been excited by her, at times almost out of his small mind. Whereas she treated him with contumely, never for a moment allowing him to forget his place – a hewer of wood and drawer of ale-casks. It may be that he saw me as no more than a bird of passage and, once flown, his time might come.'

The banker considered this possibility; it did not please him and he added, 'On mature reflection, that is hardly likely.'

Mr Ardvaak stirred. Up-river he already could hear the oncoming Chicago train slackening speed as it approached Palisades. 'And will you ever return to this Mrs Isabella Bull and her Fusilier and the lad Jonson?' he asked.

'Not a day passes but I long for that,' Henry Farewell answered. 'Though in my heart I know that nothing could ever be as it once was and that I should always be a stranger as I was then and find, as I found before, that a man cannot slough off his country like a skin.'

Trailing its plume of smoke along the farther bluffs, 777 passed.

From that fiery September morning at the railroad depot until the July night when, after the so-called Battle of Pollocks Crossing, he fled north towards the Canadian border, George Gidner did not stray further than a dozen miles from Palisades so, sadly, was never to realize his dream of America the Beautiful. Indeed, years afterwards, tapping a packaged holiday colour-brochure, he would say wistfully, 'I should have liked to have seen these Grand Tetons. And look here – this Painted Desert and, here, this Petrified Forest. Las Vegas! At night! What an absolutely splendid sight it must be. Like fire in the sky! And Death Valley, Disneyland! And so forth . . .

'But for me, the United States was Palisades and, more particularly, Henry Farewell's house and my room there. Yes, that was my America – that one room with its black hole of a closet, divan bed, hard chair, the rickety card-table he lent me to mark exercises on. Oh, and the steel engraving of a youngish woman angel flapping across a cheap gold frame. And yes, there was a plaster dish of glass apples and pears; it was a great bother to me because it had to be shifted to the bed whenever I used the table. "Take the greatest care of this," I was told. "It is Miss Turton's most prized possession." And – shall I forget it – that almost human deck-chair with CONEY ISLAND FUN PARK INC. stencilled across its back. It used to wander about the room during the night. Yes, really! I was always falling over it. Perhaps it had walked to Dakota.

'The American climate suited me down to the ground; hot air from a boiler in the basement blew up through a hole in the maplewood floor so I only had to drag that canvas chair above the grille to lie in a stupefying euphoria. Denied by pauperism of a sight of Wonders Further Afield, this gentle heat on my bum will always be America's Supreme Delight. My most tranquil hours in the New World were spent there.' (And in chill British parlours, his face would glow remembering them.)

'The big rambling house had been artificially divided and my room's walls were cardboard thin and

55

this encouraged exploration without stirring an eye-brow. Behind one wall, the one furthest from my Oxbow window, lived two women sales-clerks. By Jove, I picked up plenty from that pair. Their hurdy-gurdy voices wailed daily-diaries at one another, the principal character being the store-manager, a chap by the name of Roscoe. Could have been his first name: it's all they ever called him. Anyway, this Roscoe was a humdinger, a truly Great American. I got to know Roscoe well. He provided for a wife and five kiddies. Also his mother and mother-in-law had piled in on him. And an aunt and uncle. And there was me too; I felt part of his extended family.

'Roscoe sang tenor in the Lutheran Choir, voted Republican right down the line, as a boy-scout had visited Yellowstone Park and seen a bear, had been nominated Reserve Most Natty Dresser by his gradu-ation class at Silver Creek Consolidated School, Montana, sold hailstone-insurance to make ends meet, wore sneakers to ease his flat feet which smelled and had to be powdered between the toes before his wife would let him into bed. (He also had sour breath.) To his credit he was utterly faithful, although sometimes he rubbed up against my neighbours in the not so skimpy as all that sales-gangways and, whilst his wife was away at her grandpa's funeral, he had pressured the girl with the voice like a rasp to drive out to a chicken-shack but, once there, had behaved like a southern gentleman, only seeking to kiss her hand on the Farewell doorstep. A wholly admirable man! The archetypal *Saturday Evening Post* American! Bully for Roscoe!

'No, no, I never set eyes on him. Nor the two sales-

56

clerks. You see, of a morning, I'd gone off to eat at Mr Stavros's Kwikbite whilst they still were tearing at a cinnamon roll on their beds' edges. And I already was basking on Coney Island when they got back in the evening. But that was only a part of the action. There was another pair of Americans above me. Saw them neither. This man (it had to be a man) plodded back and forth until the early hours. And this is interesting: each time he stopped, a woman screamed. Mind you, not a big scream. More of a yelp. Then he set off on his travels again. Well, no, I can't explain it. Odd though, wasn't it? But then, foreigners *are* odd.

'So, all in all, at a stretch, you could say that, like Walt Whitman, "I heard America singing, her various carols I heard". Toilets gushing, a boiler door's clang, whispers edging past Mrs Turton's bed, and on up the stairs, the steady trudge, the small scream . . . and there I was in my cosy hive with the United States stabbing out signals at me. So, although I never saw America the Beautiful, well, many a traveller has crossed and recrossed that great land and learned less, oh very much less of the strange and savage race who dwell there.

'And, now and then, at the oddest times, Henry Farewell's bassoon surged forth.

'You may never have heard a bassoon on its own; it makes a gruff sort of noise, like an old chap ruminating on a full stomach and then belching. He used to give us,

> In the gloaming, O my darling.
> Think not bitterly of me . . .

57

'It's one of their parlour songs. Perhaps he was mourning his runaway bride. Who knows? But, more often than not, the household was favoured with "Red River Valley". Ever heard it? No?

> From this valley they say you are going,
> Yet linger awhile e'er you do
> And remember the Red River Valley
> And the maiden who loved you so true.

Rather touching? He once told me they sang it at his mother's wedding.

'Ah yes, the house itself – what did it look like? Well, like every house in town it was timber-built. This particular one was shored up with a yard-high foundation of rocks from the river. You went up a couple of steps and then across a flyproof porch and found yourself in an immense gloomy foyer, a sort of no man's land which had passages and stairs leading to everywhere else in the warren.

'This foyer was the lair of the Mrs Turton I mentioned. She may have been Farewell's aunt or his half-cousin or just somebody he'd bought with the house. Never found out. She had a murphy-bed; that's an alarming contraption which springs back at the wall like a rat-trap. (When you're not in it, of course.)

'That old girl gave me the willies: she painted her face a doll-like mask which always smiled. And there was this horrifying smell of decay. Whenever we met, she used to pipe, "When are you British going to pay your dollar War Debts, young man? Have a nice day." And cackle. After the first fortnight I didn't bother answering.

'Well, there you have it – the Farewell Rooming House. My America!

'Then why did I leave Bradford?

'Why indeed!'

To his credit, George Gidner flinched but did not back off from the novel performance daily exacted from him.

First thing each morning, his right hand pressed on the top left-hand pocket of his hacking-jacket, the other raised in salute, he directed his eighteen-year-old students to pledge allegiance to the flag of the Republic. He then called his class register, gnashing and mangling a bizarre index of Vecchios, Schwarthofs, Wipfs, Kruschevs and Zwanzigers, whilst their discomfited owners sweated and cursed their ancestors.

This done, Mondays, he relayed Principal Moskvin's mimeographed 'Start Our Week Well Message'; Tuesday, Counsellor Baedecker's Behavioural Guidance Theme, ('Your girl-friend's father, friend or foe?', 'Bad breath, face spots, causation and amelioration'.); Wednesday, Inspirational Reading furnished by the local chapter of Daughters of the American Revolution; Thursday, The Kiwanis Club's, 'This Week's Great American'; Friday, Cheerleaders' Chants ('Are yuh rootin' for our guys, Yeh, Yeh, Yeh! Fight a little harder, eh!')

Then, with half an eye on Breitmeyer's *Sentence Diagramming made Easy*, he set about the bread and butter task of tearing asunder his native tongue and laying its writhing entrails across blackboards for subslicing by his students, several of whom were a deal better at this butchery than himself. He never found this surgery less than repulsive, yet it is illuminating that his metamorphosis into becoming neither English nor American coincided with an increasingly savage proficiency at diagramming their shared language into dative clauses and dangling imperatives.

'No, I never discovered why they did it,' he later admitted. 'But they did it damn well. But that's the American Way isn't it? They make a thorough job even of gibberish. All you need to say to an American is, "That's It. Everybody else does It. You wanna be a reglar guy, eh? Then you do It." And he does It. Towards the end of my time there (I say this with modest satisfaction), I became so good at their blasted ritual slaughter that one honour-student (as I knock-ed out his middle-stump with a sharp break-back elliptical-proviso) paid me the Supreme Compliment, "That big British slob! Who does he think he is? Goddam Shakespeare!" '

His American Literature Course was agreeably less taxing – he merely had to work his way through a thick book in a blue cover originating from the Principal's store-room. And though he never developed patriotic zeal enough to fire his students' breasts during their mutual study of George Washington's long-winded Farewell Address to Congress or the geographic expertise to keep them on track as Long-fellow's star-crossed Arcadian sought his Evangeline, he made as decent a job of it as many a native-born American.

In fact, his chief affliction was not teaching but its American appendages and, whereas his colleagues, knowing no better life, were conditioned to crack-of-dawn faculty meetings, evening compulsory discussions, selling frankfurters at school football games and so on, they hit George hard. And then there were the daily directives gushing from the office. Not until Henry Farewell explained, 'Interrupt our paper-flow and we Americans begin to think (and usually ill),' did he realize that these memoranda/directives/exhortations need not be read, let alone acted upon.

But, even so, accustoming himself to Time's accumulated observances, suspicious colleagues, Moskvin's excessive sittings-in on his lessons, was not easy and there were times when these occupational waves and billows might have engulfed him. But he fought back with true Yorkshire grit and again and yet again surfaced, clinging gamely to whatever debris drifted his way and defiantly crying such slogans as, '*In statements expressing futurity with no promise implied and in the First Person Singular use "shall"*', '*In compound sentences employ a comma previous to the noun when the subject is inclusive of the secondary part.*'

And many was the time he stubbornly announced identity on yet another Monday morning by affirming stoutly, '*In clauses expressing willingness, determination, resolution, desire or promise, "will", "shall", "should", are obligatory in the 2nd, 3rd Persons Singular!*'

And to sustain their emissary on the lone prairie, each month the Bradford Education Committee transferred seventy-eight dollars to Henry Farewell's Bank.

When eventually it tumbled to the faculty of Palisades High that George was poorer even than themselves, they became reasonably well disposed towards him and began to pass him up and down the line for meals. And he repaid this hospitality by demonstrating his skill at eating peas from the back of his fork, chilling their blood by accounts of black English winters without central heating or a public performance of the multiplication of £178 19s 11¾d by 57. And they thanked him by explaining such rewarding features of native life as discounted meal punch-cards and the Sears Roebuck Catalogue, warned him against Socialists, poison ivy, divorcées, skunks, union-organizers, Easterners and job tenure hazards likely to arise from hay-riding with nubile students.

But when self-interest conflicted with kindness . . . ah! None explained the local custom of allowing students to sit-in on a course for a week before signing on for the year, nor that this trial week must be made murderously burdensome to notorious idlers and disruptives. So not only was he saddled with his fair share of recidivists but unwittingly recruited from other classes a sump of students so infamous that, seeing his posted lists, the Grover Cleveland faculty blanched. The captains of this hellish horde were his landlord's droopy daughter and her consort, an ox-built thug, Bosey Swatt, son of the town's most expensive physician.

He found no succour. Hadtlestadt, Speech/Debate (his neighbour), told him, No, you may strike neither her nor even him. No, you cannot exclude them from your room. Yes, you may refer them to Behavioural Guidance Counsellor Elmer Baedecker.

And Baedecker briskly returned them with a psycho-analytical questionnaire:

62

1. Do you eagerly await Monday morning?
   AFFIRMATIVE/NEGATIVE/UNAPPREHENDED

2. Does your teacher consistently undervalue your potential?
   AFFIRMATIVE/NEGATIVE/UNAPPREHENDED

3. Can a girl be normal and overweight?
   AFFIRMATIVE/NEGATIVE/UNAPPREHENDED

4. Do you believe geniuses often are insane?
   AFFIRMATIVE/NEGATIVE/UNAPPREHENDED

and on to 100 (of course).

And, when these had been leisurely processed, George was invited to a snug refuge far from the dust of battle, greeted with a grapefruit smile and told, 'Ambrose and Rebecca conceivably may have a small adjustment problem (which I do not necessarily concede). And if this is so (which by strict definition I cannot acknowledge) you may well find a palliative way, way, down deep.' Counseller Baedecker paused like an intelligent tracker-dog.

'What about having them last period each day and having a little dig?' George asked hopefully.

The glad smile faded and a cold voice from behind it said that it would just love to visit with such grand vital kids (from two of our community's most highly regarded families) but the philosophy of our Grover Cleveland High was inflexible; teachers must work out their little problems in a classroom context. And another sheaf of questions was pressed into George's hands.

He paused at Hadtlestadt's door. The speech expert was beating time to his class's chant,

'Pre-shrunk sheets, terrifying tissues.
Does this shop stock short socks with spots?'

'Have you tried prayer?' he was asked. 'Pray that the bird-brained no-gooders will snuff it taking an earth-correction bend too fast. I lost three stinkers doing just that on the highway north of Smolensk: there's a beaut there.'

'The sixth sheik's sheep's sick.
The sheep of the sixth sheik's sick.
Sick is the sixth . . .'

At the month end, reacting to parental complaints, Principal Moskvin informed him by letter that the School Board gave him seven days to assert classroom control. And, after gloomy calculations on the back of an envelope, George sought a parley with Bosey Swatt.

The youth grinned. 'Heard from Moskvin, eh? Ten bucks a month, mac!'
'But I only make seventy-eight.'
'Ten!'
And ten it was.

Seventy-eight dollars a month had been disabling: sixty-eight was crippling and George Gidner abandoned his last native rite, an egg and bacon breakfast and, at the Kwikbite counter, settled for an eighteen-cent bowl of branflakes (into which he furtively mulched a pat of butter which came free) and a cup of coffee. This, supported by a Hershey bar at mid-day, kept him going until about nine each night when the Parthenon café ground up any pork, fish, beef and hamburger likely to go off before morning and, at a dime a dip, ladled the conglomerate upon thick hunks of gravy-impregnated bread.

And thus it was that one early autumn night found him loitering in that steamy spot hungrily eyeing a richer man forcing a jet of mustard into a frankfurter bulging with meat. Stavros's brother-in-law perfunctorily wiped the grease from the inside to the outside of a glass, then slouched to where, in a cubicle's corner, an Okie drifter willed himself invisible.

'Not an all-night shelter, feller,' he said casually. 'Out!'

In the twilit backroom, a student couple clinched-shuffled to a nickelodeon rattling, 'Life is just a bowl of cherries', a coffee dripolator hissed, the gristle-grinder snarled. And Bosey Swatt with Becky Farewell, bursting in from the night, flung themselves upon stools and yelled, 'Hiya, Mr Gidner, sir. Three malts, Sam. And make Mr Gidner's a spiked-special.' And slapped down money. His money? George wrapped his college scarf twice round his neck against the blast and plunged through the door. The Okie huddled against a wall; the café's lamp sank harsh shadows into gaunt cheeks and below deep-set eyes. George reluctantly pushed a quarter into his hand. A face stared blankly back.

A damp breeze stirred the trees, loosening leaves and blowing them across his face. Summer's over, he thought. Somehow I've got to get through winter. Then it will be spring, then summer, and I can go home.

He made his way back across the railroad tracks. Through undraped windows he saw the pastor of the down-at-heel gospel hall contentedly comparing

65

grocery prices in *The Prairie Plow*'s pages, a woman treadling away at her sewing machine, a high-school girl connected to a telephone, an old couple munching a late meal. I've been here a couple of months, he thought, and I'm still a stranger. I shall always be a stranger. There's nothing for me here. I should never have come.

'Then . . .' (years later he made quite a song about this) 'Then a most extraordinary thing happened; my mood took on a voice – a plaintive wail, rising and sinking on the wind. I'd never heard anything like it. Quite eerie. Could only have been from the sky but when I looked up, well, there were the girders of the town's water-tank. Nothing else. But then (and only for a moment) the clouds ran clear to reveal this astonishing sight – a wavering line of big birds buffeted by the wind, each clinging to its place as they wheeled above the lights. Then clouds hid them once more. But I still could hear them crying.

'It stirred me. No other way of putting it. Stirred me! Almost to tears (if that's not going over the top about it). And I told myself not to be such a blithering self-pitying idiot. It was for moments like this that I'd come to Dakota. This was an American thing. True there were oddballs like H. Farewell, plantation overseers like Moskvin, K.G.B. bullies like Gorkev, monsters like Swatt. But also there was this. And this too could only happen here. In America.

'So I turned and went back to the café and said, "Look here, I'll have that malt, Bosey: I've paid for it." It shook them rigid.

'And when I emerged again, I felt a different chap. No, it wasn't that spiked malt; it was those birds, that

66

American thing. Well Bosey, I thought, Our Day of Reckoning is round the corner. And that will be an American thing too. Yes, I definitely recall thinking *that*.'

Next day, he told Hadtlestadt about it.

'Mr Gidner,' he replied earnestly, 'what you witnessed, sir, were Canada geese flying south to winter on the Gulf. And Mr Gidner, yes sir, those birds were confused, mistaking our town lights for water. And Mr Gidner, yes, it is indeed an American Thing and all true patriots with hearts not swinging bricks (and number me with these) are stirred likewise.'

And did he not know that Saturday, tomorrow, was the first day of the State Hunting Season and that now and for four weeks, not just pheasant and duck but man would look fearfully at man? For had he not observed the numerous citizens with missing limbs, nor that even he, Hadtlestadt (most cautious of men), was short of the tip of his third finger, left hand? And come the morrow, he, Hadtlestadt (who he hoped could be looked upon as a friend), would be around very early to have him witness this great American festival of slaughter of man and bird. Yes sir! That he would!

(And, meanwhile, Henry Farewell, heedless of the passage of the airborne fleet and home from a lonely Homesteader Hotel supper, heeled off his shoes, pleasurably crumpled his toes and shuffled contentedly to his bookshelves. *Pamela? Humphrey Clinker? A Hebridean Journey? Rural Rides? Robinson Crusoe? The Mayor of Casterbridge?*

He took down his *Tristram Shandy*:

67

"Nay, if you come to that, Sir, have not the wisest men in all ages had their hobbyhorses? And so long as a man rides his hobbyhorse peaceably along the King's Highway, pray, Sir, what have either you or I to do with it?"

'Exactly! Well put! My own opinion!' he murmured. 'Who but a boor could suppose other?'

*　　*　　*

'Do I remember the Plains? Who could forget them! They were *Dakota*. Walk half a dozen blocks and you were face to face with Out There.

'How could anyone *forget* them? They seeped in. The people I mean. On Saturdays. They sidled from sagging flivvers. Chaps in patched dungarees and caps like basins. The women . . . well, I still can see their sunk-in faces. After a couple of weeks Out There, they needed buildings to block the sky and some bustle to swallow the silence.

'No, I've not forgotten the Plains. Never shall. Or that awful mood of insignificance they brought on. And for all their honky-tonk, the Palisadans felt the same. That endless sameness Out There sapped even their smug self-esteem.

'And once that goes, anything can happen.

'Why are you grinning? Anything can happen. You still don't understand, do you? That's what Pollocks Crossing was all about.'

Next morning, George Gidner was awakened from deep sleep by peremptory tapping on his side window and, stumbling up to peer into the blackness, saw Hadtlestadt's face flattened at the pane. He pushed up the sash.

'Let's hustle, eh,' urged the speech expert. 'Us men aim to be around Olafsen's Slough before duck dawn. And for godsake keep your voice down; let's not alert Hen Farewell, eh. This I shall explain later.' And, as George wound round his neck the long striped scarf which his mother had knitted, he added fretfully, 'And say, in these United States we gun ducks down. Not strangle them, eh.'

So, still stupefied by interrupted sleep, George half fell through the window and was squeezed into the first of the three waiting automobiles. At high speed they sped along the northbound oil highway before lurching off along grassy section-lines to fan out on foot around the shallow water. There, lost in the darkness, they watched the slough lighten to reveal a huddle of migrant wildfowl. And, as the sun nudged above the prairie's rim, duck sheltering in the marginal reeds stirred uneasily and began to swim in crazy zigzags, until one squawked hysterically, flapped down a runway and took off. Then the sky was clamorous with birds fighting their way through bursting gunfire, and George, greatly alarmed, flung himself to the turf, falling bodies thumping around him. The onslaught lasted no more than two or three minutes, yet when the survivors had re-grouped into a blurred cloud beyond shellshot, it was light enough to search the grassy humps and hollows and heap the gay corpses into the car trunks.

Then they drove off eastwards to gather for breakfast in the lee of a haystack overlooking corn country. The immense fields swayed in the growing heat; farms, barns, windpumps, dwindled into mirage. Far off, dust puffs marked the passage of hunters travelling along dirt roads, seeking remote sloughs where wildfowl might still be idling.

'Where are we?' George asked. 'Has anyone a map handy?'

'Who wants a map out here!' Coach Amunsden exclaimed. 'Here in s.d., we all know where everything is and if we don't, we know There will be just like Here. This is the State where man can look furthest and see least.'

'Hey!' Hadtlestadt interrupted, 'Hey, gimme those glasses. Hell and it is too! That's Hen Farewell's Caddy no more'n coupla sections distant and coming on real fast. For pete's sake, let's get outa here. The season's no more than a coupla hours old so he can't have shot his licensed quota of humans yet, eh. That guy's a widow-maker,' he confided to George, as the convoy lurched off. 'Two seasons back he peppered Coach Amunsden so now the poor guy don't need a touchdown to cause him to leap. Farewell's gun goes off just by thinking.'

High above, wavering lines of geese moved south across the brilliantly blue sky; a huddle of pelicans exploded from a haystack. And they jogged across section after section of husked cornstalk towards their far-off marker, a red grain elevator by the railroad at Smolensk. At midday they tumbled out into oven heat.

'Diggsville,' announced Hadtlestadt.

There were no dwellings, no street. Only a bank. It said so in bleak carving above the shattered door. BANK OF DIGGSVILLE. A cracked concrete path led from its collapsing portico through a tangle of weeds to an overturned car chassis.

'Coupla elevators down by the tracks hung on longest,' Hadtlestadt told him. 'Then they burned. Bye, bye, Diggsville.'

Around them aching miles of corn stalks poking up from the dust, faded grass, cracked earth, the sun a fire in the sky. 'First settlers named it AQUA,' he went on wryly. 'Aqua! Ha!'

And it was there, amidst Diggsville's departed glory, that Henry Farewell, fondling his twelve-bore shotgun, found them. 'Is it not true, Gidner,' he asked, 'that in your country only the very wealthy hunt?'

'You have to buy a horse, then learn to ride it,' George said lamely, noting that his companions were scattering and, although unsure of the precise nature of his peril, he began to sweat.

'How very revealing!' his landlord exclaimed in high, clear tones whilst moving closer. 'Yes, of course, your aristocracy hunt on horseback and shoot on foot.'

His gun went off with a stupefying roar. Two far-off pheasants catapulted from the corn. George fell on his back.

'Good God!' Amunsden whispered. 'He's shot the poor devil.'

But Hadtlestadt held his arm. 'No, no, I was observing closely,' he replied calmly, 'but do not move. Stay quite motionless: there still is a shell in the breech. You will see that the Englishman will get up presently. He will only have lost his power of speech, eh. It was very brave of Gidner. He didn't bolt like the rest of us. My old grandpa (on my mother's side) also was an Englishman.'

And it was so. George bent a brief horrified glare at his attacker and tottered off. And, in the awed stillness, the hunting party heard the banker exclaim, 'How very extraordinary! I do apologize, my dear fellow. But you will bear me out – my finger was not on the trigger.'

'I think that I shall walk home,' George told Hadtlestadt. 'But first I shall rest here awhile.' And he sat quietly on the Bank of Diggsville's steps until the coast was clear.

Great heavens! he thought, I might have been lying stretched out on this filthy counter whilst they haggled a Best Deal with the mortuary. What a pretty penny it would have cost Dad to have had me shipped back to Bradford! Deadweight!

Then, taking a rough bearing from the sun, he set off south, then east, up and over folds of grassland and shallow gullies until he reached and slogged along another dirt road. An automobile slashed past, its passengers staring back incredulously through its trailing cloud of grit. Then another. It stopped.

'Hiya, Mr Gidner, sir!' It was Bosey Swatt and Becky Farewell. 'Like a lift?'

'No, no,' he replied. 'Taking a breather. Stretching my legs. Enjoying a stroll in the country. Mustn't delay you. Kind of you to offer.'

'A stroll! Whereya strolling?' the youth asked with studied interest.

The question struck George like a hammer blow. He was a foreigner, an oddity, a long-stay tourist, one who *strolled*. He cracked a wry smile. 'Oh, nowhere in particular. Just out for a countryside walk, you know. Isn't it delightful weather?'

He convinced neither himself nor them. Yet when Becky giggled, Bosey Swatt snapped her into silence and stared reflectively after the shambling figure. (For a brief moment he even considered reducing his monthly exaction.) And that night, his father was shocked enough to exclaim wonderingly, 'This afternoon something happened which our son strove to comprehend and was pained because he could not.

73

From his garbled utterances, some incident concerning his English teacher. But he has been *thinking*. Thinking! Is that possible?' (But his wife, knowing that he secretly blamed her side of the family for their son's thickness, feigned sleep.)

The incident had significance too for George Gidner: he had been close to retreating into the town for the rest of his year. But now, fixing on a distant building as a marker and, in an access of sheer bloody-mindedness, he stumbled across a single-track railroad and ploughed off into a cornfield black with grasshoppers. In the stillness he swore that he could hear their jaws inexorably devouring the dying cornstalks whilst multitudes more lay stupefied in the dust, their glutted bodies bursting obscenely under his tread. I am in the Great Drought, he thought. This is Another America. This is Out There. O.K. O.K. So what! I can take it.

Far off, two young farmers, the Murrays, staring bleakly across their land, watched the wayfarer. Fifty years earlier their grandfather had painfully homesteaded this quarter-section and their father had laboured a lifetime maintaining a hold. And now it was slipping from them. On the kitchen shelf behind the clock was wedged a bundle of bills for fertilizer, gas, machinery, hardware, feed, lumber – bills which could never be paid. This was their last year.

But when, at last, turning slightly south again, George saw the watchers, he saw only two far-off men loitering on a grey desert. He had not travelled far enough yet from Bradford to see more than that. But, that afternoon, something had happened of which he was yet unaware. Not much, but something; the beginning of a lifelong *affaire* with the Dakota plains.

An hour later, he reached the crest of the Bitter-root's bluffs.

The lone building, his marker, was now no more than a quarter-section distant. A dirt road plunged past it, crossed the red meccano bridge spanning the shallows and raced steeply back to the plateau and away towards Palisades. No one moved on the vast landscape.

He idled on the slope watching the river loitering past a herd of Hereford steers loafing knee-deep at a ford. Then, turning again towards the west, his eyes followed a line of telegraph posts and sagging wire back to this building. In town, he would have passed it without a glance. But here, utter isolation gave it significance.

He got to his feet and trudged along the bluffs.

It was a double-fronted rural store, its twelve-pane windows separated by a half-glass door and fronted by a long open porch whose roof wavered on six frail pillars. This sheltered in its shadow a rocking chair and a backless school bench. Approaching closer, he saw that its second storey was a false front supporting only a flagpole, a single window shamelessly revealing the sky. Before it, the road had been widened so that wagons and now automobiles could swing round. And across the gravel, overlooking the river and on a low concrete plinth, was a bulky something wrapped in a roped tarpaulin. And by it a collapsing bill-board:

Now he was near enough to read the store's exuberant inscription:

POLLOCKS CROSSING
POPULATION 1
Elevation 362 feet
GROCERIES: DRY GOODS: HARDWARE:
Medicines: paint: flour: Guns.
BOOTS AND SADDLES.

LIQUOR had been painted out but was re-appearing.

(And, later, he sometimes said, 'I couldn't believe in it as a commercial establishment. I mean to say, it was as if it had been lifted across my path by some wizard and, like a childhood tale, would disappear when I turned my back. Airy fairy? Well, perhaps so but bear in mind that I'd had a harrowing day and that it was very hot.')

He entered. Chewing a splintered cigar, the store-keeper was seated behind his counter on a high stool. The old man's hair was white and combed forward to his brow, his face was dark and deeply creased. He was blind. 'Sir?' he said cautiously.

'I'm quite thirsty. Parched in fact. Anything you have – coke, lemonade. Oh, anything.'

'James Ardvaak's the name. What do you look like?'

And Mr Ardvaak, rummaging beneath him, came up with a black and not too clean jar.

'Look like? Oh – quite ordinary I suppose. Perhaps

a bit on the large side. I'm twenty-five. Good Lord, what is this stuff?'

'Call it "Old" myself. Brew it up in the backroom but don't holler that from the housetop. And you're an Englishman.' He twitched an armband and twanged it.

'Met up with another Englishman way back. Spear-fish. Long ways west of these parts. Over beyond Big Muddy. In the Hills. Law officer. Came in on the Cheyenne Stage. Swore to uphold justice and put down vice. Weren't no more'n two, maybe three hours in town and he comes spinning outa Joe Lick's Saloon like a Abyssinian humming top. Too far gone. Couldn't help him any. Same manner of speech as yourself. Disremember his dying words.

'Put it down real slow if you're legging it back to town. Anyways, heard tell of you from Henry Fare-well. Speaks well of you. Drives out here most weeks. Brings that horn of his. Says he needs quiet and quiet needs it. Sound sure carries a long ways out here. Woman in Birdswing Township claims she heard him playing "Red River Valley" a coupla weeks back. Tend to believe her.

'Me? Come here as a youngster. Sod house no more 'n fifty paces from this store. No more'n a hump now I guess. Wandered out west, ten, eleven year till my folks passed on. Tracked back and took on the homestead. Lost every last cent when Shanklin's Bank went bust.

'Shanklin started up a new bank so went to town to get my money back. Scarf over my face. Empty gun. Reg'lar hold-up artist. Things going fine. Bank folk froze. Then this darned cashier, Easterner, passed over his trick drawer. Bottom fell out. Alarm goes off. Half Palisades out hollering. Rip off scarf. Bolt into street. Yell, "Hold up in there folks." Crowd jams bank doors. Head outa town. But that cashier musta clumb out toppa folk's heads. Grabs a rifle offa Jeff's Hardware. Lets fly. Misses me. Hits steering-wheel. Ricochets. Never seed since. Now you know all that's worth knowing.'

'Your telephone is ringing,' George said.

'Ain't deaf. Party line. Lucy Stringer's call. Mine's three short and a long. Jury rules Not Guilty. Henry Farewell's Dad stakes me out here at the Crossing. That cashier snuffs it back East. Ulcer caught fretting over other folk's cash.'

'Remarkable!' George exclaimed reverently, mentally filing the details for his *Brief Lives* and, as they took up their mugs and moved to the porch, examining a large square hole cut into the store ceiling.

'Heat downstairs gets upstairs that way,' Mr Ardvaak said. 'Bed stands over hole. Knew what you was looking at. Can hear folk's necks twisting.'

They sat in silence. George felt that he had known the storekeeper for a very long time.

'Some days get a glimmer when I look full in the sun. Believe one day when it's hot on my face, I'll see again. Think it could be so?'

George considered this, said that he understood what Mr Ardvaak meant and that more unusual happenings had come to pass.

'Well, don't care all that much,' the old man said. 'Get along real good notwithstanding.'

'That yellow stone on your watch-chain?'

'Sutter's gold, Mr Gidner. Ella's Bar, Sacramento.

Forty-niner traded it for silver pocket watch my Uncle Edgar give me. Chimed the hours. Now you're going to ask me what was I doing in California, ain't you? Was a little chap in Illinois, young feller in California, grown man in Wyoming, Montana and then the Hills. Ain't but a few main streets west of the River I've not looked along one time or other. Taos, Jubal, Salt Lake City, Sheridan, Smith's Hole, Sundance, Cheyenne, Laramie, Idaho Falls, Pocatello, Hot Springs, Payette, Epiphany, Sagamon . . .' The names rolled on . . . 'White Horse, Grey Bull, Deadwood, Big Sandy Stage Station, Gold Reed . . . seen 'em all in my day.

'Now I'm an old idiot out here on the Plains.'

They were silent, their faces turned towards the prairie. Far off, farms and barns pushed up like driftwood, farmland washing in around them. Here and there a scatter of trees, boughs bitten off by drought and frost, punctuated the miles. A freight train crawled over the landscape.

But neither saw these things. They looked back and across a panorama of the Great Days when each settlement lay across unmapped distances painfully traversed on saddle or coach, when wayfarers crept like insects in a gigantic wilderness, each huddle of dwellings a landfall.

'Seen 'em all,' Mr Ardvaak murmured. 'Tagged on a line of folks inching along by Springfield Court House, Illinois. Man hoisted me up. Looked down. Long feller in pinewood coffin. This man says, "Some day, son, tell your kids you seed Abe Lincoln. Say you saw him fetched home." '

George gawped at the gulf of time yawning before him.

'No!' he exclaimed.

'I seed Abe Lincoln,' Mr Ardvaak said with shattering finality.

George downed the last drops of Old and stood up to go. 'That tarpaulin over the road,' he said. 'What's beneath it?'

'Cannon.'

'Good gracious! Why?'

'Traded in my Aunt Susie's longcase clock. Considered it would look real elegant out front. Expect I shoulda asked where that trucker hauled it from. Wanted rid of it too bad to have got it legit. Guess he snatched it for scrap fronta some town hall back East. Henry Farewell swears it's a genuine Revolutionary War gun. Hobby of his. Oughta know. Always egging me on to let him put it through its paces. Tell him it might blow up. Would surely miss his society. Pollock? Who was Pollock? Trapped beaver I've heard say. His kids seed insides neither church nor school. When them and taxes moved in, he moved on.'

He cocked a sightless eye at his visitor. 'Come again,' he said.

On the crest of the bluffs going down to the bridge, George Gidner paused and looked back. His face turned towards a harsh sunset firing the plains, Mr Ardvaak sat stiff as his cannon's ramrod.

And when he had crossed to the southern bank's bluffs, and was more than a mile along them, he turned again. In the last light, the store at Pollocks Crossing stood stark, like a stone raised by a people who once had known these parts and were gone.

*   *   *

'Good gracious! Wherever did you dig this up? And whoever took it? Hetty Jo? Becky? Pass me my spectacles. There by the tea pot . . .'

Mr Gidner peered at the three men staring stonily from the faded snapshot.

'Mr Ardvaak!' he muttered. 'Older even than I remember him. And Farewell! Heavens, yes, that extraordinary suit! It had four buttons and he did up all four. ("I wear it only on Occasions, Gidner, my dear chap.") Well, what Occasion was this, I wonder? And that marvellous bow-tie. Blue! No, black! Black with red spots! He does look rather grand, now doesn't he?'

For a long time he looked in silence at the third figure, the blank face, club tie, braces, pipe clamped between teeth.

Did he will that solid shape to step from the picture, to speak, to say, 'Yes, this was you'? To ask, 'Who am I now . . . What has become of me?'

Mr Gidner passed back the photo. 'I would rather that you hadn't shown me this,' he said. 'Tears come easily to an old man.'

'You have asked so I shall tell you,' Henry Farewell said, looking across at the bridge below and settling happily into Mr Ardvaak's rocking-chair.

'Miss Bull, Bella, was a nonpareil, James. Believe me, a California grapefruit inspector would have graded her Top Quality. Both fore and aft. In fact, it occurred to me that the financial fate of The Fusilier hung on an exciting possibility that, some unforgettable evening, her costume would split and her

81

essential glories burst forth. Remembering her I can only quote and reverently,

> Return, return, O Shulamite,
> Comely as Jerusalem,
> Terrible as an army with banners.
> Return that we look upon thee.'

And for a few moments he was silent in a lost paradise. 'Sadly, America no longer breeds such women,' he said.

'On my first night there I lay in a backroom overlooking an orchard which went down to the river. River sounds at night! A delight denied us prairie-dwellers, James. And, lying listening, I supposed myself utterly content.

'Then – and it was the most startlingly marvellous moment of my adult life – then she was with me. One moment by my bed, her robe slithering to the linoleum, the next slipping like a fish into my arms. On my *first* night! It was inordinately flattering to a man of my years. And what do you suppose she said?'

'Love me, Yank,' Mr Ardvaak suggested sardonically.

'She said – "Tell me about America." In bed with a stranger! Tell her about America! Well, I hope that I showed no astonishment: after all, I am a literate man. (There are similarly unusual situations in Richardson and Fielding.) So I answered that America was a land of bewildering topographic variety. "As are you, Miss Bull," I ventured to add. "And there too may be found delectable hills, honeyed valleys, dusky woods, gushing springs . . ." (with her giggling like a schoolgirl as I pursued the analogy up and down her). Ardvaak, that woman! She urged me on with wild exhortations and I am happy to report that I rose to the occasion.'

Once more he was silent.

'And, when we were done, she turned on an elbow and said as deliberately as if buying fish, "Am I really like America? Me? Really, Mr Farewell? No kidding?" "Yes, yes," I assured her. "You are, you are. A gloriously exciting, tempestuous continent!"

' "Well I never!" she exulted. "Then you are my favourite explorer." '

Mr Ardvaak laughed quietly.

The banker looked quizzically at him. 'I see that I need not explain why I did not trudge around Westminster's tired monuments or take a snapshot of the Changing of the Guard.'

Mr Ardvaak laughed again.

Fall in Dakota is a lovely yet melancholy season. Sunlight is still brilliant but the wind is thinner, more persistent. There is no body of water in the creeks, sloughs dry out, groves of yellowing trees pattern the faded distance. You ring the soft-coal man and invite him to top up the heap in your boiler-basement each time he passes; at night you wrap your wife's moulting fur coat around the automobile radiator; you make a deal with your neighbourhood grocery to feed you until spring; you hope to read in *The Prairie Plow* of violent storms in Florida where your sissy brother-in-law has sought refuge from advancing age; you face up to community campaigns with a rock-hard resolve not to be elected to anything. Then you sit back, vow that this winter you will read the Twenty-five World's

Great Books and, in the new year, emerge a New Man.

And when, one grey-blue November day, winter came to Palisades, first in a flutter, then with two days and a night thick with driving snow, this same fall lay locked beneath succeeding snowfalls until February's end so that the Bitter-root froze a foot deep and the ice-factory thriftily moved out and chain-sawed the river.

Then domestically dominant matrons basked at home whilst their husbands outfaced the elements, staggering and sliding from house to car, to office to car, to store to house. And on the white wastes beyond the town's last dwellings nothing moved but withered sunflowers tapping at walls and windows or tumble-weed hurrying over drifted fences and round ice-capped fodder-stacks.

And Henry Farewell explained to George that Dakotans' lifestreams deepfroze till the spring thaw, that this was the cause of their longevity and that numerous East Coast eggheads had been living in great comfort and ease for years on foundation grants to research this phenomenon.

So the iron weeks passed. Christmas-tide came and went. And, on the first day of 1930, the banker hailed the yet distant spring by installing a flashing-sign,

THE SETTLERS' BANK,
BANK OF STRENGTH AND SERVICE.
ANOTHER YEAR HAS COME,
LET US GREET IT WITH JOY.

When the semester's end approached, George, implementing Principal Moskvin's Philosophy of Suc-

84

cess, sensibly arranged for all his students to succeed. Well, all but one. What madness suborned his reason as he flunked Bosey Swatt will never be explained satisfactorily.

The tidings spread swiftly.

Still in basketball squad strip, the youth galloped into the session room, checked the list, tore it down and advanced menacingly upon George.

'Change it,' he grunted. 'No one flunks me. No one. Let alone a damned foreigner.' And slapped down the paper. 'Right now, mac.'

Alarm having deprived him of utterance, George could only shake his head.

'Change it. And fast.'

'No.'

The youth struck swiftly at George's face, missed, lost balance, fell across the desk and before he could right himself, his neck was gripped tightly.

George now rose to exert more weight and, gathering inspiration from the Class Motto above him on the wall (BEYOND LIES THE TIMBER. NOW LET US BUILD), allowed Bosey's head to rise three or four inches before cracking it back on the woodwork, repeating this exercise with increasing emphasis whilst he chanted savagely,

'Are you rootin' for the boys . . . Yeh! (Crack)
Are you makin' plenty noise . . . Yeh! (Crack)
Fight! Fight! Fight! . . . Yeh!' (Crack)

then unexpectedly released him but, hustling round the desk, gripped his wrists and pushed out a furious face so that they almost rubbed noses.

'And there will be no more handouts, you gorilla,'

he hissed. 'And if your screwball girlfriend gives me trouble, be you as pure as driven snow . . . And bugger my job.'

A profound struggle raged inside the youth. Then he muttered, 'Sorry!', turned and went.

Head in hands, George Gidner sat for a long long time. Then he got up, pinned the crumpled list back on his board, drew a red ink circle round Swatt's indictment and despairingly waited for Swatt's parents' denunciation and Principal Moskvin's execution.

He was wrong. A few hours later he received a note from Dr Swatt.

I have examined with unusual interest my son Ambrose's head and my diagnosis is that education has had its first measureable effect upon him. At long last he understands that the case Passive Intransitive can be modified by Active Intransigent.

I would be happy for him to have extra tuition in simple math and, let us say, general civilized conversation. We could discuss remuneration for this admittedly onerous task.

Once more, allow me to express my admiration for this striking effect on our son's welfare.

How astonishing, he marvelled. The Americans really *are* foreign.

But this was not the only spin-off from this violent episode.

He was sleeping deeply when he became aware that someone not only was on his bed but crawling into it and atop of him.

'It's only me,' the visitor said in a surprisingly firm voice. 'Me – Becky.'

'Get out,' George hissed. 'And keep your voice down. Get off me this minute, you ridiculous creature. Have you not heard of the Mann Act? Are you bent on getting me jailed? How dare you, you horrible delinquent!'

'Aw, gee, Mr Gidner, don't be prissy. Not after what you did to Bosey! Here I am. To the victor the spoils!' And she set-to eating his face and groping elsewhere. This triggered a near volcanic upheaval and, even as she was picking herself up from the floor, a violent knee jab at her bare bottom shot her through the door into the black foyer.

He then softly recited,

'By the shores of Gitche-Goomie,
By the Shining Big Sea Water,
Stood the wigwam of Nokomis,
Daughter of the Moon, Nokomis . . .'

After a time, he fell asleep.

All this time, the unknown American in the room above had been pacing steadily. Now he stopped. And the woman gave a small scream.

When, next evening as they strolled aimlessly on the town's outskirts, he lamely reported this passage of arms, Henry Farewell begged to be spared further elaboration and apologies. 'It is true that Rebecca is my child,' he said. 'That cannot be disputed. But she is quite beyond control. As was her mother. I can only proffer my sincere admiration at the upright way in which you handled the vexatious situation and beg you to forgive her. Perhaps,' he added (with no confidence at all), 'her visit was no more than a bizarre interpretation of apple-polishing – it is common knowledge that you daringly have re-introduced F-grades into our High School.

'But, apropos the regrettable affair, would you not agree that the sexual impulse is one which affects us deeply and each must make arrangements to cope as best we can with its miserable necessity? Take my unhappy self . . . my Alyce was enough for me and I supposed that, for my part, I pleased her. I was mistaken. So what was I to do when she went off to Colorado with that salesman of dreams? A woman's consolation is not a devouring appetite, yet neither am I without a taste for it. Palisades will not tolerate bordellos, so what must I do? Believe me I am not overproud that each couple of weeks I invent a business conference in Sioux Falls and go off with a sales-girl, Hetty Jo, disguised by a typewriter.'

He shook his head (perhaps mourning this furtive pursuit of happiness) before continuing solemnly, 'You make no comment. However I am touched by your confiding in me, since you must know that American myth will have our female young as inviolate as the Roman vestal virgins, and that school boards and the Law are suckers for their lies. But Rebecca can be relied on absolutely. Of this I have her assurance. (Though doubtlessly she means to try again. So either you must bolt your door or accept her simple offering. And if you care to regularize such an arrangement, I should be happy to have you as my son-in-law.)'

'Thank you, Mr Farewell,' George replied, not

unmoved. 'That is jolly understanding of you and you can rely upon it that I have told you the whole truth. I cannot afford a wife, so I shall buy a door-bolt and deduct it from my rent.'

The banker appeared not to have heard him.

'Her name is Hetty Jo,' he sighed. 'Tomorrow I shall take you to my store and introduce her to you.' He blushed. 'Between ourselves, Gidner, I think of her as The Delectable Mountain. You recall your Bunyan? And the shepherds whose flocks grazed upon it? When you meet you will understand. Now, for a few moments, let us rest here on the bleachers. You can go through the laws of cricket yet again whilst we observe our High School football squad rehearsing. Why do cricket players protect their legs and fingers but not their heads?'

('Winning is not *Everything*,' Coach Amunsden was roaring. 'It is the *Only* Thing. Kill! Kill! Kill!')

'Tomorrow evening we entertain Huron High,' the banker murmured. 'This is the pre-match Hate Session. I do not need to explain that he does not mean *everlastingly* kill. He only is suggesting some mild buffeting and gouging in the Pit.'

'The pit of the stomach? Really!'

'No, no, the Pit is the thick of a scrimmage. The helmets are not merely brain-shields. They convert heads into missiles. Let us move on.'

('Kill! Kill! Kill!' yelled Amunsden.)

'Now you were telling me of a cricket referee's last wish to be buried in a white coat and grasping six pebbles. Why a *white* coat and why *six* pebbles? But your mind is elsewhere, Gidner.'

'Should we not hurry to that poor man's assistance?'

asked George, who had observed a respectably dressed person crouched astride an enemy and, gripping both ears, beating his head upon the paving slabs.

'No, on no account,' Henry Farewell cautioned. 'It is merely a trifling postscript to last week's Storm-Sewer Vote. Here, in Palisades, a public project needing minimum capital expenditure of 2,000 dollars must be voted upon by all taxpayers. The underdog is Mr Nordner who lives in the N.E. Ward and thus is connected to our 1924 Storm Sewer. His assailant is his brother-in-law, Mr Fullenwiezer, who lives in the S.W. Ward where, each spring thaw, his basement fills with putrefying effluent from the John Adams Grade School's urinals. Until the overflow subsides he is forced to evacuate his family to his wife's parents' home in Smolensk. Need I explain that yet again the majority of taxpayers have rejected increasing their tax bills by the expense of an extended sewage system. Normally the two are the best of friends; he certainly will stop short of killing him. Even in this current access of passion he only hates Nordner in a general sort of way. It is little more than a manifestation of our democratic process.'

They walked on until Nordner's feeble cries could no longer be heard. 'By the way, Gidner,' Henry Farewell cautioned. 'A dead cat . . . never handle a dead cat: it could give you diphtheria.'

*   *   *

'Yes, yes, nod your head. But you don't understand. You live in Another World. They popped you aboard at Sioux Falls and, less than twelve hours later, here you are in my landlady's parlour. And tomorrow they'll squeeze you out on Palisades air-strip and none of your pals the wiser.

'Look – I was eight days getting there. Eight days! And then there were ten months without the county cricket scores, a decent cup of tea, a shower of rain, an English voice. And I was young. Only a year or two older than you. With an uneasy foothold amongst foreigners.

'I was damned lonely. The whole business was a disaster.'
Mr Gidner filled his pipe and smiled bleakly.
'And I did it to myself,' he said.

The Dakota spring does not sidle in, half-demurely, half-reluctantly, like spring in England: it explodes with suitable American violence. Friday, bare trees, a fringe of soiled snow in the north corners. Monday, green buds, heat bouncing from sidewalks. Instant spring!

And, driving east to visit Mr Ardvaak at Pollocks Crossing, Henry Farewell pointed out a woman firing a cover of thistles left till the last minute to hold down the soil. Her husband's plough stirred puffs of dust.

'Ah, Gidner, I fear that this spring must be the end of the line for many of these poor people,' he lamented. 'As well plant sorghum in the Sahara as plant it here! For five years this land has yielded no more than three bushels of small grain to the acre. Three bushels!

'And we bankers and the loan companies push them hard and, all too often, over the edge. And, when we foreclose, we sell for no more than a repayment of taxes. I have let farms go to town physicians, merchants, teachers, to anyone who can afford to let the land lie fallow till better days. I feel vulgarly conspicuous driving this Caddy.'

He rubbed his flimsy moustache and looked at the fiery sky. 'Three families from this one township moved out last fall – the Norstadts and the Maclintocks back to their folk in Iowa. The Massingers drifted west, hoping for seasonal work in California (our new Canaan) – for the first time in their lives without a home!'

On a dirt intersection line they turned south and then west, bumping along a grassy track until they reached an abandoned farmhouse, its sagging fence lost in a sunflower thicket. By a broken wheel and a smashed barrel, a sign read:

COURT-ORDER SALE FOR DELINQUENT TAXES.
McCormick Mower, John Deere Cornplanter,
Rock Island Cultivator, J.D. Gang-plow,
Aspinwall Portable Planter, Hoover Potato-digger,
De Val Cream Separator

They pushed open the door.

'See, Gidner,' he said. 'The end of an American dream.'

On the living-room floor lay a scatter of trash – a worn-through galosh, a cheap handbag, a headless doll, a cracked lamp and, legs stretched in an agony of starvation, the skeleton of an intruding jack-rabbit. Charred in the stove's hearth, a scatter of chattel and mortgage reminders. And letters from the old home in Illinois. George picked up one:

> I am glad you are all well and we all pray you get some rain. I am sending you a bedspread, and thank you for the nice card and handkerchief but you didn't need to spend your money on me. We only hope you have rain and can raise something this year. Here, the apple trees are in bloom and trees leafing out and it won't be long before everything will look real nice . . .

'These Massingers were one of the first families to homestead out here in the eighties,' the banker told him. 'Alexander Massinger proved up another quarter-section as a tree-claim.' He nodded towards where, a few hundred yards distant, the great barn had fallen in upon itself; gaunt trees, whitening down from their tops, were dying in the drought. 'That would be Massinger's grandfather.'

They left the house, pushing through shoulder-high sunflowers. 'And, Gidner,' he went on, 'here is a small thing, a mere detail but one which may interest you. For your literary work, my dear fellow . . . Look. See – there. And there. Look how the turf has sunk. In the old days there were no rural cemeteries and town burial rates were steep. So many a settler knocked up a rough box and dug a grave close by his house. Maybe a priest or a minister would call. Perhaps a neighbour would read a few verses from a testament. Then they buried their own.

'See how tiny they are, these graves of children. I have heard it said that Massinger's father had two sisters. It would be summer, in the heat when fever thrived. You know how it is with children – beyond saving in a few hours, gone before even the physician rode out.

'Think of it, my dear fellow . . . each time the mother stood at her kitchen door, she must have cursed this bitter land, longing to return East, yet not bearing to leave behind her children. And now . . .

'Yet perhaps it does not signify, Gidner – being forgotten, I mean. I was shown this place and now I have shown you and who is to say that, some day, you will not return and stand where I stand and tell another what has been told you? And so on. It is better than a stone wearing away in the weather. And here is one more thing that I must show you. And with shame. A notice of foreclosure, last nail in hope's coffin.'

He held out a faded paper.

THE SETTLERS' BANK
President – Henry B. Farewell.

. . . mortgage now due and unpaid $10,565.45 and $25 attorney's fee will be foreclosed by sale of said mortgaged premises to the highest bidder at the front door of the County Courthouse on 31 August 1929.

Then they climbed into the automobile and drove on to Pollocks Crossing. The banker dawdled off to the bundled up cannon. 'One day you must see this, Gidner. It is in absolutely mint condition. A really splendid example of one of the last run of barrels turned out by the Warwick Furnace, Chester County, Pennsylvania. Cast brass and not a day younger than 1772. Think of it! This may have been one of that obdurate battery on Five Furlong Ridge which discouraged your General Burgoyne from turning our lines at Saratoga. On that Great Day when Ardvaak agrees (as he will, he will) to my charging and firing a July 4th Salute, I should have valued your services as my gunner's mate. An Englishman! Perfect! But, alas, you will be gone.'

On the store porch an unshaven old man, bolt upright, occupied the school bench so they went inside and seated themselves by the unlit stove.

'Edward Hastelow,' Mr Ardvaak told them. 'It's Edward Hastelow out there on the porch. Deafer 'n post. Comes Fridays. Has for years. Picks up his groceries, sits awhile, then tracks home. Don't talk any. Been shut up inside hisself since the nineties I've heard tell. Lost his intended then. No more 'n week to the wedding.'

'That was a long time ago,' George said.

'Prairie fire. Biggest ever in these parts. Came in on a steady west wind. Tumbleweed spread it. Rolled over fire-breaks folks ploughed around their places those days. This Hastelow's intended – no more'n nineteen. Name of Susanna. A Massinger. Fine, long-legged, black-haired girl. Had bright eyes. Them that recall her always say that. "Bright eyes! She had bright eyes." Taught school at Clara Township.

'Her folks seed her running. Hitched up and headed out for her. Missed her in the smoke. Backtracked and come on their girl at night. Lifted her screaming into the wagon. Wind had died. Her ma was holding a candle in her hand. Still as that. Burned black as an African. No eyes. Fed her spoonfuls of water.

'Them that seed her, prayed for her to die.

'And on a Sunday she did.'

George glanced at Hastelow sucking his pipe. Most of his teeth had gone; his deepset eyes gazed at a private world.

'Does he ever talk of it?'

'Never to me. Maybe never to nobody. Daresay might have been better if he could have. Never moved away neither as folks said he oughta. Never heard tell of another woman. Ma, pa, all the Massingers, all of them that loved her, over the years he's seed em all go. Come winter he tracks around in a raccoon coat down to his ankles: no city hunter's winged him so far.'

'She had bright eyes . . .' His words struck at George Gidner's fading purpose, his *Brief Lives of the Frontier* and destroyed it. For this was the moment when once magic names took on a rancid flavour – Poker Mamie, Billy the Kid, William B. Hickock. Paranoid, bird-brained butchers! They were without substance. Shadows! And sank into shadow.

That girl running for her life through smoke and flames, racing to a safe island of ploughed earth, breath failing, legs dragging. Then the fire was upon her.

These almost anonymous pioneers, families from settled states outfacing appalling loneliness, back-breaking toil, an unpredictable future – these were the true heroes of the frontier. And here, on the spreading farmland around him, unsullied by roman-tic concoctions, evidence of their way of living was waiting to be gathered. Soon it would be gone. And it dismayed him that he might have returned to England with no more than a catalogue of diseased fiction!

That same evening he burned the sheets of his *Brief Lives of the Frontier* (Preacher Smith and All) in the basement furnace and, overnight, became the historian of Teddy County.

And to the end of his days he was never to forget that bright-eyed girl, running, burning, falling. And a candle flickering across the night.

The father of one of George Gidner's students was a primitive American who, fearing that if his motherless daughter was not home by nine o'clock then she must be heading for the sin-struck East, forbade her to bum around in boyfriends' automobiles. And, purchasing a bicycle, he made her ride it. 'Furthermore,' he unkindly added, 'this will wear down your waist.'

She was not a bright girl but genius touched her briefly. At the close of a day's session she approached George. 'Gee, Mr Gidner, Sir, all the kids admire your historical researches. Yes sir! And we all declare it a real big shame you having to roam around those dirt roads on your own two legs. So, Mr Gidner, Sir, I want you to feel free to borrow my bike when you wanna go outa town. Gee, Mr Gidner, you can have it all weekends and no call to hand it back Mondays. Yes sir! A Tuesday will be fine. Or for that matter, a Wednesday. So long as I have it back Thursdays. Then you can have it Fridays.'

George was touched.

And that evening whilst her dad was walking the dog, she telephoned her dearest friend. 'Clever little bird-brain me!' she exulted. 'They both fell for it, the big mutts. Yes sir! Two-Gun Gidner, the Desprit

Diagrammer, told me I was a generous and warm-hearted young lady. And Old Belly-Acher drooled he was real glad he'd brought me up to venerate my teachers nor scorn our fathers whose ploughshares broke the plain. And, now that he had evidence of me growing up, I could stay out till 10 Saturdays and 10.30 Sundays. Yeh! That's all he'd raise it. But it's a beginning.'

Thus, Out There, George became a familiar sight grinding the pedals and stripped to his braces (but never leaving off his collar and tie), until even kennelled hounds no longer howled at his passing and farmers, touched by his eccentric concern for their grandpas, passed him up and down the section lines.

'What's this?' he would ask, and what looked like a harmonium turned out to be an ingenious corn-planter and what should have been a mantrap was sworn-to for a hayburning stove with a twister attachment. He didn't argue. 'They should know,' he told Hadtlestadt. 'It was their grandads'. Mine could read the *National Geographic* and stayed home.'

So now, in his new role and in full flush of enthusiasm, he improved the time by joining the County Historical Society. On his first visit, befitting a scholarly occasion, he wore his dark suit and was pleased to find that Henry Farewell and Mr Ardvaak (who had been brought in by a neighbour) had similarly observed the proprieties. Present also were such notables as Mr Draper of Draper's Slough, Mr Tolstoy of Tolstoy Township and Mr Bowdle (whose memory the State Cartographic Department would keep green at Bowdle Creek, Bowdle Sluice and Bowdle Grove).

The advertised speaker was a Mr Little Cloud, an ancient resident of Pine Ridge Reservation far beyond the Missouri. He sat motionless, gazing inscrutably at a patch of wall slightly above the audience's head-line and George entertained an interesting speculation that he always had been there and the Courthouse built around him, that it had been this lofty indiffer-ence which had provoked White Americans to an exasperation only assuaged in the blood of their hosts.

Mr Little Cloud was introduced, his biography lightly sketched in, his standing in the counsels of the Oglala eulogized. Not an eyelid flickered. For several moments he stayed silent. When, at last, he spoke, his harangue in the Sioux tongue was fired at his audience in harsh bursts (each single-clause sentence, George noted with approval, rocked on its heels by an immovable full-stop). Between each crackling verbal volley he paused and stared bleakly before him whilst Mr Charles Feather, a town Indian, shuffled ner-vously and essayed a mild, conciliatory translation, cravenly dissociating himself from the speaker's opin-ions by beginning each instalment with 'He says . . .'

The two voices went implacably on, each in its own way telling with terrifying inevitability how Mr Little Cloud, as a child held at his mother's saddle-bow, had witnessed the Battle of the Greasy Grass, how George Armstrong Custer and the 7th U.S. Cavalry, lured deep into the Little Big Horns, were there savagely cut to pieces in the wild charge of Red Cloud, Crazy Horse and the riders of his ruined nation.

The homesteaders listened gravely.

99

The old man fired a last burst at the ancient enemy. For several moments, nervously rubbing the palms of his hands, Mr Feather pondered the words. And when he spoke, the deprecatory tone and 'He says' were gone. He, too, gazed bleakly above their heads as he intoned harshly, ' "The long-haired one, the fair one, their captain, lay slain in that place. And his brothers lay beside him. Our fathers turned. They rode away. It was done." ' Ah, thought George, this was the victory which doomed his people and he knows it.

A few more years and there would be a bloody vengeance in the snows of Wounded Knee.

But Mr Little Cloud was not yet done. He lowered his gaze, looked fixedly at George and, raising a hand, uttered an incantation. His interpreter looked puzzled. 'It is poetry,' he explained apologetically. 'It has nothing at all to do with our Speaker's advertised subject. It goes something like this:

> Swift and far I journey,
> To Sisnoyinni and beyond it,
> To the holy place and beyond it,
> To life unending and beyond it.'

He looked rather resentfully at the phlegmatic historians but, recalling that when Little Cloud had returned to his reservation, he, Mr Feather, would have to make a living selling insurance in Palisades, added winningly, 'Well, folks, I guess what he really means is that he's feeling pretty old.'

The evening was brought to a close by a whistling solo rendered by Mrs Bowdle. This was received with loud and prolonged applause.

*

The following Sunday, Henry Farewell suggested that they should drive westward to the ranges beyond the Missouri. 'It will not do, my dear chap, for you to see only the prairie farmland. Your uncles and aunties will chide fretfully, "What no buttes? No arroyos? No Buffalo Bill? No Redskins! Then, in heaven's name, why did thou chuck away good brass on thi' travel ticket, lad?" '

So, taking a sack lunch, they set off. It was a propitious morning, a deep blue sky, the earth green with false promise. A couple of hours later they crossed the shifting sandbars of the great River and raced up and beyond its bluffs, so that, before their onwards rush, the landscape unrolled to a blurred ruffle of far-off hills. 'I have heard it said,' murmured the banker, 'that once beyond Big Muddy, one has crossed the threshold of the True West.'

(And long years later, George Gidner would lament, 'Ah Dakota! I shall never forget that first sight of ranchland and range, spreading like a fan to the Black Hills and over and on to that dreamland beyond Wyoming – the snowy Tetons, Idaho's Snake River, Silver Creek, Golding's Post, Santa Fe, Taos . . . but even then I knew that I would never see those magic places and that My America was to be dried creeks, dust-drifted highways, an arid town, a rooming-house on Oxbow. Sad! Terribly sad!')

They hurried on . . . Green River . . . Seven Troughs . . . Gooseneck . . . Faith . . . Nightingale.

('Sometimes, half watching a TV Western a spread of country like that poor Farewell and I crossed that Sunday rolls across the screen and I can barely sit it out. It tugs at the heart.

'Can't describe it otherwise. As bad as that! And I feel that I can't stick this town, this tamed country for another day, another minute, that I must grab a suit-case and rush off, go to see Dakota as I saw it that blue, hot morning. No, don't tell me. I know it. I know it wouldn't, couldn't be the same. But that's how it is and that's how it always will be with me. Well, let it pass, let it pass; how can you be expected to understand.')

Vivian, pop. 167, empty lots like lost teeth . . . Murdo, pop. 58 . . . White River, 43 . . . Parama, 5 dwellings and a bus-stop . . . Vetal, 7 and a gas station . . . Patricia, a café and a church (too bulky to haul off) marooned in tall grass where streets once crossed . . . Bates . . . fork south for Pine Ridge, fork north for Wounded Knee.

They halted at a scatter of patched ramshackle shacks amongst dying trees: a single cracked bell clacked a call to matins in the Episcopal Mission Church of the Holy Cross. An aisle divided men from women. George glimpsed Mr Little Cloud: he still was gazing stonily before him.

The service wandered casually along, amens were grunted, responses uttered, a sermon received without notable edification. But for the brown skins, black hair and bright eyes, a service-book in two languages, the two travellers might well have been in Bradford or Palisades.

Then why, why did a colder wind blow through that final hymn? A sugary tune, a child's catechism verse,

> We are but little children weak
> Nor born to any high degree,

> What can we do for Jesus' sake,
> Who is so high and good and great?

But an old lady began to wail and, in next to no time, they all were going hell for leather, *'Manito! Manito! Manito!'*

But this was no mild harbinger, no pursuer of peace. This was a Messiah armed at all points, hoofs hammering in bloody pursuit as past galloped savagely across present. Manito! Manito!

The harmonium trailed into an uneasy silence; the congregation resumed its immense indifference.

Mmmm, just so! George thought. 'The long-haired one, the fair one, their captain, lay slain in that place. And his brothers lay beside him. Our fathers turned. They rode away. It was done.'

He followed his companion into the sunshine and watched as the Sioux climbed into wagons and drove off: the presence of visitors had not been recognized.

As life drained from Wounded Knee's short street, the two climbed a little hill where, beneath parched grass, lay the mass grave of the Minneconju Sioux, Big Foot's straggling band of sick and starving people.

> *Many innocent women and children*
> *who knew no wrong, died here . . .*

and a roll call of frozen corpses shovelled into the dread pit,

> *Wounded Hand, Red Eagle, Scatter Swift Bird,*
> *He Crow, Young Afraid of Bear, Yellow Robe,*
> *Ghost Horse, William Horn Cloud . . .*

Then they got back into the Caddy and drove homewards over the range, recrossing the Missouri to the farmland until, like a great white bird, a Trans-Continental crossed above, making for Huron, Minneapolis and the distant seaboard. Far off, the town water-tank marked their jaunt's end.

'Last week, you were telling me of your English Wounded Knee, Gidner,' the banker said. 'A place named Goosepastures, I gathered. What an absolutely splendid name! The enclosure of public lands by your aristocracy and the hopeless resistance of a Captain Pouch and some few ill-armed peasants . . . You remember? I should appreciate hearing the end of that story. This evening, after supper, perhaps? At a quarter after nine, shall we say?'

'Miss Bull was what I fancy might be termed a peasant, James,' said Henry Farewell when, next evening, he turned up at Pollocks Crossing. 'The great Chaucer would have understood her perfectly. She could figure and (I use her terms) cipher. This is true. Otherwise, formal education had left little discernible trace. Reluctantly I must report that, had it been left to Bella, the nation's musicians, painters, poets, need never have lived. Her favourite song epitomized her Rule of Living and, at least once a week, she had it strummed on the piano in her Snug and sung with an excess of feeling by a poor down-and-out who was rewarded with a pint on the house.'

' "A pint on the house," ' Mr Ardvaak murmured dreamily.

'Her regulars put up with it. No, I am being unfair:

many appeared to derive some aesthetic pleasure,
perhaps even moral reassurance from the words.

> In the world, I've gained my knowledge
> And for it I've had to pay.
> Though I never went to college
> Yet I heard the poet say . . .

Which poet was never made clear. But he must have
been a man of some spiritual certitude,

> Life is like a rolling river,
> Flowing on from day to day.
> Men are vessels tossed upon it,
> Sometimes lost and cast away
> (Chorus) So then do your best for one another . . .'

'Practised what she preached,' Mr Ardvaak
remarked drily. 'Between the sheets.'

The banker considered this interpretation: it did
not please him. 'She had a big heart,' he eventually
conceded, 'as well as a big bosom. If our arrangement
was pleasing (and I have no reason to suppose that it
was not), it was because she knew that I was deeply
interested in her as a *thinking* person. I *listened* to her.

'And for her part, for one who had received minimal
schooling, it was quite remarkable how she exerted
herself extending mine, insisting that I must see more
of that England which lay beyond the charmed
borders of her bar and bed. "You really need a proper
guide, an educated know-all," she told me. "But you
must put up with whatever drips and drops I've
scraped together."

'But I could not have had a better mentor. You see,

James, like William Blake, she had preserved that rare childlike wonder of seeing things as it were for that first exciting instant.

'Shall I ever forget the trip we made to Stratford-upon-Avon!

' "This spot was started up by Shakespeare Bros.," she told me. "That fat chap I showed you crouched up the church inside wall handled the business end. And the thin creep with the big head over on yon pillar in the flower bed, he was the one they go on about – the bookwriter."

'Alas (and I deeply regret this) I stupidly hinted that the randy Buddha and the careworn tycoon were one. She did not dispute it; merely said, "Tell me then, why have they given him two heads?"

'James, you see what I mean? The nub of it! Unanswerable!

'During a country walk one evening, I recall venturing to ask, "Whom do you suppose me to be? The essential Me?" (Knowing Bella Bull, it was the bravest thing I have ever done.) Well, she did not answer for a longish time. Then she said, "Because you have asked and only because you have asked, Mr Farewell," (and she still persisted in emphasizing the second syllable). "You are not what you may think you are. But some blessed day you will find out and then God help those close by."

'Now James, as one "close by", what do you suppose she meant? And indeed what if she was right?'

He did not appear to expect an answer and, when he spoke again, he already was on another tack. 'She had a genuine concern for my welfare,' he said.

'Far beyond the call of commerce,' Mr Ardvaak said drily.

'You deliberately misunderstand me,' the banker said testily. 'I was thinking of intellectual rapport. For instance, I recall most vividly an incident on that same evening. We had gone perhaps no more than a couple of miles from Minden when she stopped and leant on the top bar of a field gate. "Now," she told me. "Heed this meadow."

'So I leaned my elbows on this same gate and examined a herd of Jersey cattle cropping the grass. They were sleek beasts. But neither redder nor sleeker than those over the next hedge. I waited.

' "Yon's a battlefield," she said. "My Old Dad told me as his Dad told him. Underneath them beasts dead men lie. But no use to look for a stone or for mention in books because the chaps that shovelled them in wrote the books and put a stop to stones.

' "It was to do with Property, my Old Dad said. First the top dogs swallowed the abbeys. Then they wiped their greedy chops. Then they pushed up their plates for the left-overs. These being no more than the holes and corners where us Bulls and suchlike ran a few pigs to see us through the winter. Then they got their lawyers to swear to this and sign for that. Then it was theirs. The lot!"

'(Ah, James, how that young woman could tell a story!)

' "But not here in Goosepastures," she said. "Here it wasn't a walkover. Yonder, two or three hundred folk swore to fight it out, toe to toe, come what may. But when it was down to brass tacks, some got cold feet and never came and some ran home, till maybe there was no more than a couple of dozen stuck it out. And three women.

' "And they were poleaxed like pigs."

'I ventured to suggest some monument, perhaps a wayside cross. In fact, I went so far as to offer to pay for such a stone. But Bella would hear nothing of this. "No," she said. "*They*'d stop it. And it happening three hundred years ago makes no difference to *them*. *They*'re still there. And will be till the end of Time."

'Ah, James, now can you not see why, on memory's page, that one rough meadow holds more significance, more excitement than a legion of Olde Beefeaters propping up Ye Tower of London? For me that field, Goosepastures – I shall remember it till the day I die.'

And, unconsciously, he touched his breast.

By this time, George Gidner's American Literature Course had wound its way well into the nineteenth century, come to grips with Henry Wadsworth Longfellow and, having disposed of Evangeline's lover vainly shuttling the Southern States seeking his beautiful Arcadian betrothed, he turned gratefully from that implied denunciation of British colonial tyranny to Hiawatha, the aboriginal Boy Scout, who from his birthday by Gitche-Goomie, through an honourable wooing of Minnehaha, Laughing-Water, to his day of departure into a tranquil sunset, stooped to nothing that was not cricket.

His class's eyes shone: this was an O.K. coloured American and Becky, mourning that he wasn't around, irritably hacked Bosey Swatt's shin and didn't say why.

' "One race indivisible!" Ah, but really it wasn't like that,' George pontificated. 'Let us reflect upon the Black Hills, Paha Tipi, sacred ground of the Sioux nation – until a strong smell of gold was traced to its gulches. Ah, then how briskly a solemn treaty was revoked! And we must reflect on an unarmed Crazy Horse bayoneted whilst a guest of that same army he had scattered in the Little Big Horns. And what of Sitting Bull, a priest of sorts, murdered in his own tepee, his body, dug up by night, carted off for a tourist attraction?

'And we must look long at Wounded Knee and a forlorn band of women, children and old men straggling through bitter weather towards Government guaranteed shelter at Pine Ridge. Then cut down by machine-gun fire, left dying in the snow. A fine revenge by the Seventh Cavalry! And, to compound the crime, Presidential award of eighteen Congressional Medals of Honour. Honour? Honour!

'Let our Hiawatha paddle off into his sunset. But not his people! They dragged themselves off to degradation. First butchered, then starved, now neglected. "One race indivisible"! Ha!'

The session bell saved him from further madness.

Next day he was summoned to Principal Moskvin's office. Present were two members of the School Board and the Grand Commandant of the local American Legion Post. A hatchet job took no more than a couple of minutes. With warnings of sterner measures if he indulged himself in further un-American eloquence, he too went off but into a far from tranquil sunset.

*

He was not kept waiting to be shown his betrayer. Next day, the English session had scarcely begun when Gary Gorkev, the police-chief's son, rose. 'Mr Gidner, about what you told us about the Redskins . . .' he began.

'Ah, Gary, but that was yesterday,' George answered, withdrawing in good order. 'A new Day has dawned and we find ourselves on p. 314 with the great Lincoln holding forth at Gettysburg. Doubtlessly you recall my invitation to commit his deathless words to memory's page. And, as you already are on your feet, yours shall be the honour of reciting that declamation. "Fourscore and seven years ago, our fathers . . ." Go on from there.'

'About Wounded Knee,' the youth persisted. 'I talked it through with my dad and my dad said . . .'

'Tell me when class is dismissed,' George said. 'You wouldn't want to use your fellow students' precious time. "Our fathers brought forth upon this continent a new nation conceived in liberty . . ." Resume there, Gary.'

'My dad said it was a battle.'

'And I said it was a battle, the Battle of Gettysburg. "Conceived in liberty and dedicated to the proposition that all men are created equal." If we go on like this . . .'

'Wounded Knee! You said it was a massacre; my Dad said it was a battle. And on our State Map it is marked as one – the Battlefield of Wounded Knee.' And he dramatically flapped out a coloured sheet and stubbed a forefinger at it.

George gritted his teeth and hung on.

'Well, Gary, that is your father's opinion. If he and

the State Governor claim that it was a battle, that is their democratic right. It is what Gettysburg is about. Go on from, "that all men are created equal".'

'But you told us it was a massacre.'

' "Upon this continent a new nation conceived in liberty . . ." '

'You said that the U.S. Army massacred the Redskins at Wounded Knee.'

Even as George Gidner turned at bay, he felt warning hair rise on the nape of his neck. 'If the State Map says "battlefield", then the State Map lies. I am convinced that it was as shameful butchery as that of the Macdonald Clan by my countrymen in the Pass of Glencoe. And that also was in the snow. There, you have what you wanted. Ah well . . . "Now we are engaged in a great Civil War, testing whether this nation or any other nation so conceived and so dedicated can long endure. We are met on a great battlefield of that war . . . a new birth of freedom . . ." '

The bell rang, his class dispersed.

' ". . . shall not perish from the earth." '

He bleakly spoke the last lines to a classroom wall.

There was an emergency meeting of the School Board and, that evening, without a hearing, George was let out of the Palisades System.

Next morning he returned to his empty classroom (GEORGE G. GIDNER, INSTRUCTOR had already disappeared from the door) and when he had cleared the desk drawers and pushed the bits and pieces into his pockets went down the hall to bid farewell to Hadtlestadt. But, instead of intoning alliterative jargon, the class had been quelled into unnatural study by a fierce-looking woman. 'Oh,' he exclaimed. 'Where's Hadtlestadt?'

'Shhhhh,' she hissed and scrawled on a scratch-pad, 'HE HAS BEEN FIRED.'

'Whatever for?' whispered George.

'THEY FOUND OUT ABOUT THAT OTHER WOMAN.'

'Good gracious!'

'NOT HIS WIFE.'

She tore up the page into very small pieces and, ignoring the trash basket, carefully pushed these into her handbag.

'But he was a jolly good teacher and the kids liked him.'

'I SHALL ANSWER NO MORE QUESTIONS. I HAVE HEARD ABOUT YOU. GO AWAY,' she wrote.

And wonderingly he went.

She tore up that too.

Henry Farewell sighed when he heard the story. 'You have transgressed against a tribal taboo. The U.S. Army is our holy cow. You murmured "Boo" so you must stand in the corner. But do not think too hardly of us. Reflect how your Bradford authorities would have received an American's dire opinion of Britain's taboo – your Royal Family. But God help us – what would Tom Paine have said?'

He said this whilst lounging on Coney Island, the rising heat gently stirring his thin, fair hair. 'However it would distress me to have you starve at my gate, so I shall recruit you for my country's chosen destiny to gorge the world with goodies. Be at my Store at eight-sharp tomorrow. No, no! Merchandising expertise is quite unnecessary. Faith is all. Each day when the sun rises at its eastern gate, draw forty-eight lungfuls of our almost pure Dakota air and repeat (each time a little louder) MAN EXISTS ONLY TO CONSUME. It may be that, after a time, you will believe this. Nothing convinces a customer more than conviction. And apropos nothing at all, Gidner, does your brain ever feel as though it was boiling? Over, I mean?'

Thus it was that, next day, clad in a green coat advertising BUXKIN GIRDLES and behind the ladies' accessory display, George applied himself to selling inexpensive adornments. And when, a couple of days later, the banker's giantess joined him at a luncheonette, she bore glad tidings. 'You're IN, man,' Hetty Jo exulted. 'IN, IN, IN! Sales at your stand are way, way up. Merchandising-wise you're a dead ringer. Coupla folks called Hen to say he has the dandiest sales-clerk that ever hit town. Say, why do you call all the dames "Modom"?'

'It means, "I have a wife and six kids. Please buy something: I need the commission." '

The Delectable Mountain brooded on and accepted this. Yet, although she had a clouded mind, her heart was purest gold. 'Say, any evening you come all over you-know-what, you can count on me, Mr Gidner, sir. Purely for relief, you understand. And strictly for free. Anytime it comes on bad except Tuesday and Fridays which are church choir practices.'

George was quite touched. 'Thank you,' he said. 'And I shan't forget. But I seem to have become used to doing without "you-know-what". This may well be because I can afford red meat only at weekends. But we could give it a try-out, couldn't we? What about tomorrow which is a Saturday?'

A week later Dr Swatt ran him down. 'Can I help you, sir?' he was asked urbanely.

'You can help me by telling me your side of the story.'

And when he had heard, 'That's real bad. I've been out of town but I shall try to have your dismissal set aside at the next Board Meeting. No? Really! You have a better deal here dollarwise?'

He looked closely at George. 'How much longer will you be with us?' he asked. 'What! For no more than a month! Well, I guess we've given you a bad time. But don't hold it against all of us.'

He's a goddamned whizz, the watching Hetty Jo thought, easing her exuberant breasts on a cash register. Now him, I could go big for him. He's not a tube of limp lard like Hen. Nor does he have dental decay. Saturday, it was real good.

By and large, she was a good young woman and George Gidner might have done much worse than to have married her and begat a race of Dakotan giants. And, had he known, such a suggestion might have been favourably received because, that very week, a roving evangelist from Fort Dodge, Iowa, so stirred her nobler self that she indignantly refused further favours to Henry Farewell and began seeking employment in one-room rural schools west of the River, a region so shrunk from that no teaching certificate was asked for.

*   *   *

'And they still remember me in Palisades? I'm astonished. Yes, truly I am.

'I wrote to no one, heard from no one. It all stopped that last night at the Crossing.

'Very strange! Very sad!'

Mr Gidner drew the curtains on the darkness and rain.

The following Wednesday, Henry Farewell and George, heading across the devastated farmland towards the Crossing, came upon a bulldozer and several pickups in the yard of a rundown farm. A young man, a woman and a child huddled in the house porch.

'Alas,' the banker said. 'It is Ed Murray's place. He farms it with a brother who (to put it kindly) is not quite himself. A doctor in town, J. B. Leverecz, held a mortgage on this farm and, when repayment dried up, sold it over Murray's head. For these times, he was offered an advantageous price because an out-of-town syndicate plan to augment an adjacent section which won't be cropped until things improve. But, despite a court order, Murray refused to vacate and when they sent out a bulldozer the younger brother loosed off a couple of shells. So now the new owners have called in the Law.'

He drew in to the roadside and gazed gloomily across to the buildings. 'We took their cash for lumber, seed, hardware. And when they reached the end of the tether, we took their land,' he groaned.

A bulldozer began to push at a barn.

'I fear that Murray has no leg to stand on. In fact it will be extremely fortunate if the pair of them escape committal for resisting a court order. That their grandfather filed on the property in the eighties is quite immaterial.'

Even as he spoke a squad car came on very fast: it was Police-Chief Gorkev, ostentatiously armed.

'Gorkev has no call to be here,' Henry Farewell said. 'This is Findlayson's, the County Sheriff's, territory. But Findlayson knows these folks. Doubtlessly he has gone sick and this awful man has been called out to enforce the law.'

They watched. The young farmers, slight, sandy-haired men, were hustled from the house and bundled into a police car. The women and child were weeping.

'What will he do?' George asked. 'Murray, I mean.'

'Perhaps he will drift off, living in makeshift shelters and other men's barns, his self-respect as well as his land gone. He will have heard his father tell of the old days, the struggle for a foothold, black winters, grass fires, cyclones, plagues of grasshoppers. It is more, much more than a farm he is being forced from, so he will go bitterly, with hatred in his heart. Most of all for himself, knowing that he has lost what was so hardly won. He won't forget.'

The machine was pushing at the frame house. It fell so easily. Planks creaked, windows shattered, tar-paper gaped, shingles spurted in showers. A puff of dust, and it lay like a crushed matchbox. A dog, roped to a wagon wheel, howled.

The police-chief rose from a chair, dusted the seat of his pants and, still nursing his Tommy-gun, drove off with his prisoners. The neighbours crammed into a single rusting pickup. As they passed the banker they gave no greeting.

Henry Farewell stirred uneasily. 'And Great Heaven, to think that no more than a week has gone since I sat through a Sioux Falls banker's convention where we solemnly affirmed that only a little time after tomorrow, Prosperity will rise like the ocean's tide and cover the land. We passed such a Resolution – so now it *has* to happen. (We Americans have a touching faith in the power of incantation.) Gidner, my young friend, I like less and less the way I live, the way I always have lived and the way I was brought up to believe all good Americans should seek to live.'

He started the motor and turned towards the westering sun. Looking over his shoulder, the scene seemed naggingly familiar to George Gidner, and he recalled his long-ago trudge across the ravaged corn-fields from the abandoned Diggsville Bank and his first sight of Pollocks Crossing. Those fields were these. Those far-off farmers were the young Murrays. It had been his first visit to that Other America.

Henry Farewell was still muttering.

'It is the immensity of the sky out here, Gidner. That and silence! In town the only sound I hear is people yakking, "Look after my money real good, Mr Farewell. Make it make more money, Mr Farewell. Then we can all be happy, Mr Farewell." '

He did not pursue this depressing theme: his words trailed away.

They rode along the dirt road, dipped down across the red steel bridge and up and over the bluffs. And there was Mr Ardvaak waiting on his canopied porch.

'Glad you've come, Henry, and you as well, Mr

Gidner,' he said, rising and shaking hands. 'Been a trifle on the low side all day. Hoped you might stop by and talk me outa myself.'

George Gidner never saw the great Wonders of America nor even Dakota's own marvels – Mitchell Corn Palace, Huron Fairground, the Badlands, Wall Drug. And, quite unfairly, he never was to stand reverently before the cast-iron post marking where Joseph/Preacher/Martyr Smith fell amongst thieves.

Consolingly, excitement is relative to circumstance and, afterwards, he would recall sitting at night far out on the prairie, first hearing its melancholy jangle, then the whistle's desolate cry, as 777, Chicago-bound, a ribbon of light trailing along the water, picked up speed along the Bitter-root's bluffs. And, looking back across the years, such moments would be Wonder enough to tease and tug at his heart.

Was it on such a night, that Henry Farewell, watching its passing, had turned and murmured, 'So Gidner, my dear chap, in no more than three weeks . . .' and vaguely waved his small hand towards the dwindling lights and then across the enveloping night to the single lamp at Ardvaak's Store.

Was that the night?

They had gone on to the Crossing where Mr Ardvaak's coffee dripolator was bubbling gently on the stove lid.

There had been another visitor. 'This man here – Breitmeyer –' the storekeeper had said, 'longtime acquaintance. Salesman. Kindly give me this.' A yellow banner like a bedspread was festooned across the hardware counter and on it, in flaring letters,

'I carry Uttman's *Self-Instructor*, a home library in ten volumes,' intoned Breitmeyer, whose neck was so short that his small bald head seemed glued to his shoulders. He spoke robustly around a king-sized cigar.

The four sat in silence: Breitmeyer's self-introduction plainly had not run its course.

'East, south, west, north, like a weaver's shuttle I cross our great land,' he droned. 'No hearth, no home, no loving family awaits my coming. But where'er, from ocean to ocean, Uttman's flag flies, some fireside has a place for Breitmeyer. And of these hearths I hold this dearest to my heart.' He rattled this off without emotion but Mr Ardvaak, whilst not necessarily believing the compliment, was not unmoved. 'Few folk seed what Breitmeyer here seed,' he said. 'Never weary of the tale. Kindly tell these people, Breitmeyer.'

'Two hours after midnight on July 4th, 1925, at Lodgepole Butte in Perkins County, Montana, I visited with citizens of Another World,' the salesman rattled off, fixing George with a basilisk stare. 'It was not my custom to be abroad at that hour but I had met (and subdued) stubborn sales-resistance on the Standing Rock Sioux Indian Reserve. Then, with the north fork of the Grand River below and Thunder Butte dead ahead, I was cognizant (was aware, that is) of an illuminated object (similar in outward form to a small meteor) make a lazy loop across my windshield until its flight was arrested. (That is, stopped.)

'I therefore alighted being under compulsion (jinxed that is). As I approached through the sage scrub I observed that this thing was sitting on three legs (like an outsize plate camera). It pulsed bursts of beautiful silvery light.

'The gentleman on the staircase was very welcoming. "Friend," he said, "you may approach." (He spoke in Russian of which, because of my old grandpa, I also was cognizant.) So I did just that and there were three gentlemen and one lady. They were not green like in comic strips.

'I was given this.'

He fished out a black egg.

'Our Uttman editorial researchers (recruited from eminent Eastern colleges) state that it is not an earthstone. You may hold it, sir.'

George passed it to Henry Farewell; it certainly was very heavy.

'I then expressed a desire to make a reciprocal gift and brought Vols. 1–5 of my Uttman *Self-Instructor* sample set. But when I suggested bringing the remaining half-set, the gentleman who had been leafing through Vol. I at lightning pace said Not to bother, as they knew it all. (This also is a well-known Earth anti-sales defence reaction. He did not appear to understand that I should not be billing him.)

' "The navigational error has now been rectified," he said. "We must now leave your beautiful Soviet Union and" (favouring me with a smile) "its friendly people, and journey onwards to the United States where our mission is to discover where they dig up their extraordinary presidents."

'(I was deeply affronted by this statement.)

'Then the door slid-to and they rose into the air. For several minutes there were very nice sounds of music on the butte. Also a very nice smell.'

He stopped.

'Whatever did you do then, Mr Breitmeyer?' George asked eagerly.

'Like any good American, I drove real fast to Ralph City and alerted the Minister of the Four Gospels Fundamentalist Church. He counselled me to alert the Sheriff of Gillette County because his O.K. should have been sought before a landing and also to report the seditious remark as it contravened Immigrant Declaration Clause 8. He also said he would have wished that I had deposited a Gideon Bible with them.

'Tomorrow, I have a long haul to Dubois, Wyoming.'

'Thank you, Breitmeyer,' Mr Ardvaak said. 'And depend upon it, your booster banner will fly above this store till our wind wears it out.'

'In your travels, I suppose you have not come across a Mr Joe Braithwaite?' George asked.

'Why do you ask, sir?'

George told him that Mr Braithwaite, his mother's favourite uncle, had disappeared into the United States many years ago, promising to return. But had not.

The salesman considered this.

Then he said, 'You must inquire of him in Smith's

Ferry, Idaho.' A faint smile flickered over his face and he half lowered a reptilian eyelid. Then he bowed and left the room before George could address a second question: 'Are you the Breitmeyer of Breitmeyer's excellent *Sentence Diagramming made Easy*?'

*   *   *

'My "roughing-up"? That's putting it mildly.'

Mr Gidner touched his nose wryly.

'It wasn't this shape when I left Liverpool you know. But I'm not complaining. Discovering America was the big idea and exploration has its hazards.

'What did I discover? The essential thing?

'You fear the Russians.

'Well, I fear you.'

During the first days of June a hot dry wind began to blow steadily from the north. Like a fan from an oven it dried out ponds and sloughs and sealed the springs. Leaves curled and shrivelled on the trees, planted sudan, millet and milo scorched, then withered to little more than a fire's grey ash. Day succeeded day of intense heat. And folk of a fanciful turn of mind swore that they heard the earth ring and, as the sun rose to its zenith, that the pitch of ringing rose till it seemed their ear-drums would split and the earth's crust shatter.

Clouds gathering in the north drifted high above the plains, yet farmers no longer watched the skies but huddled in the shadow of barns or loitered aimlessly by the dirt roads. Their fathers and grand-fathers had talked of such times in the eighties; it would be like that – some would go to the wall, some would hang on.

Then, as the roots died, top soil stirred and lifted in the wind. It stripped paint, seeped into houses, into cupboards, into beds, stung skin, choked lungs. Midday was black as midnight and airline pilots crossing between Bismarck and Omaha, Rapid City and Minneapolis, reported that the prairie was hidden by a tide of dust crawling southwards into Nebraska.

This wind blew for four days and nights. And when it sank and the dust settled, fields had been scraped to the bone, roads and fences had disappeared beneath drifts, roofs of sheds and house tops poked up like islands, dead fish floated down the choked river. And there was a great silence.

About this time, an Eastern Corporation, salvaging the assets of a collapsed Cheyenne River bank, announced the first of fourteen sheriffs-sales in that district. At the first of these nothing more violent happened than the jostling of strangers whilst the debtor bought back his mortgaged livestock for a nominal dollar, the sole bid. But at the second sale fighting began when a bank nominee, having made an opening bid of 500 dollars, was set upon and badly roughed up. Five farmers were arrested and carted off to the jail at Pierre.

Within a week, during a riot on Legrand's only street, a law-officer was shot in the foot and an aged woman died of excitement. These stories were picked up by the Eastern press and brought some mild rumblings in Congress, furious denunciation from salaried, middle-class communities and, as the farm families on relief nudged forty per cent, Washington announced that the Vice-President would visit the state with a small public works programme in his pocket and a Message of Hope on his lips.

The younger Murray brother was released on bail pending trial and joined his brother's family sheltering in the Farewell Rooming House. In these uneasy surroundings, the woman and children mooched around whilst, for hours on end, the men sat morosely on the porch. In the evenings they were joined by the banker and, often, two or three neighbours from out beyond the Crossing. But as the Vice-President's visit approached, no more callers came and Ed, the elder Murray, taking his host's automobile, drove out of town each day. And each evening Henry Farewell unwontedly returned to his bank and remained alone there until the early morning hours.

George Gidner scarcely noticed what was going on around him. He made farewell visits to the few friends he had made, bought inexpensive souvenirs for aunts and uncles and looked eagerly ahead to July 5th, his day of release. America already was sinking into his past, so that with almost indifference he heard that the younger Murray brother had returned to the family homestead and had hung himself in the half-darkness of its still standing barn.

Then, withdrawing from the Settlers' Bank his astonishingly large savings of 117 dollars, he revisited the railroad depot to buy a ticket to New York and a steamer passage to Liverpool. And, whilst this unusual order was being processed, he lolled against a crate and reminded himself of this, his first view of Palisades. These were the same false-fronted ware-houses, the same mad muddle of power cables strung across the brazen sky, the same breathless heat, even the same idler (or a spitting image) on the same doorstep. His beginning and his end: the drab prospect encompassed his American year.

Nothing had changed and neither had he. That

earnest expectation of becoming a Changed Man? Ha! He recalled the wrecked Chicago gambling hall, his promising fellow traveller slipping off into the Minnesotan night, his poverty exacerbated by Swatt's miserable extortion, Moskvin's churlishness, his lost job. And Henry Farewell! He had done nothing more than live for a year as a stranger amongst an alien race whose language, by historical accident, he could understand.

It had been a lost year of life.

A railroad clerk, with a bundle of tickets, roused him. He pulled himself upright and looked along the tracks driving inexorably to the limit of the parched landscape. Then, hearing a distant bell, he lingered to watch 777 steaming in from the East. The same conductor stared unrecognizingly at him.

'QUINN ... BOX ELDER ... RAPID CITY ... ROCKERVILLE. . .' The same jargon. No one got in, no one got out.

'SPEARFISH ... TERMINUS FALLS . . .' The magic had gone sour.

Well, he thought, this is how I came and this is how I shall go. For all the good it has done me, I might as well have walked around the Roundhouse and caught the next train back east.

He was wrong. Shreds of Dakota would cling to him and the time would come when the faded plains beneath their great spread of sky would haunt him like a dream into which he would long to return. Yet never could.

On July 3rd, Henry Farewell did not return to the bank after supper. Instead, he looked in on his lodger and said, 'Ah Gidner, my dear fellow. It is more than likely that I shall be occupied elsewhere when you leave us. Our Vice-President's visitation . . . things are expected of me . . . my position in this community and so on . . . But, of course, you understand. So let us take this last opportunity of a stroll together.'

Years later, this obsessed George Gidner. 'Our last walk but as it turned out, not our last talk,' he would repeat, uneasily tapping the spindles of his armchair. 'And on a Wednesday (never a good day for me). Well, I know now that he already was half round the bend. Farewell, I mean. But I had no inkling then. How could I? In fact, it is truly amazing how reasonable he sounded. No one, no one could have guessed what was threshing around his crazy head. He might well inquire about boiling brains!

'I recall exactly the way we took – along Oxbow, passing his bank at the intersection of Jefferson and 3rd, but on the opposite sidewalk, then his store. After that, we took the route I'd trudged with my baggage that September morning I landed up in town. The Rialto Movie Theater, Vogler's Cigar Store, the Roundhouse – that way. I even looked for the spot where the drunk was beaten up by that awful man, Gorkev. But this time we crossed the tracks to the seedy blocks where they'd penned the low-income families.

'It only was when we had left the highway and were well out on the open prairie that he came out with it. "Gidner, my dear fellow, I fear that I have been something of a drawback to you. A bit of a millstone, eh? And lately, I feel you would rather we had never

127

met. Certainly things are not as once they were between us. What has gone amiss?"

'Well, how does one answer a gambit like that, half accusation, half plea? But he'd made it plain enough that he would have an answer, so I said something about supposing it was a conflict of temperaments. I was me and he was him etc. It sounded terribly feeble.

' "Ah," he replied. "That indeed may be so. Yet surely it is more than that?"

'At first I thought that I could get away without answering. (You see, it simply wasn't worthwhile; after all I would never see him again.) But of course I'd long known that I never should have been shanghaied into his house. Unwittingly I'd queered my pitch on that first fatal morning. Americans like reglar guys. And Henry Farewell was not a reglar guy; he was a queer fish. He was different. By heaven, he was Different. And I'd been written into the local scenario as "Hen Farewell's buddy". So I was Different too. All right! So be it. But, at this late stage, what sense in an inquest?

'So I tried to talk him out of it. "We're not on the same wavelength, that's all," I told him. "You wanted more from me than was there to give. From England too. The pair of us – we couldn't live up to your expectations."

'(And this I understood because it had been like that for me: I'd hoped for too much too.)

'We walked on without a word for quite a spell. I recall looking over my shoulder; the town water-tank had dwindled to matchbox size.

'Then he had another shot. "No, my dear chap, that is not quite what I had in mind. Perhaps I should not have imposed myself upon you. I certainly should not have insisted on our Conversations. But it diverted me and living here, year after year, can be tedious. But there is more than that come between us. Perhaps you are beginning to put two and two together? Perhaps sense that something is going on? Something that you want neither hide nor hair of? And you wonder if you are not in a bit of a hole. The same hole as, well, as a mad dog?" And he giggled.

'Frankly I simply hadn't a clue what he was on about. I didn't feel at all that way. Though, later of course, I understood.

'We picked up one of those grass tracks that bound some section lines instead of roads and, as we started down it, he said something that I've turned over a lot since. Quite uncanny in fact!

' "So your American Year is near its end," he said. "Now I fancy that you had high hopes of it doing something special for you? Yes? And now you are in the dumps because you suppose that it has been lost time, that you still are that same chap who sailed so expectantly into New York Harbour."

'He was talking very earnestly now.

' "Gidner, you are wrong you know. You are marked for life. Till the day you die you will carry something of those you have lived amongst here – poor Ardvaak, Becky, myself... perhaps not the Americans you hoped for but, nevertheless, Americans of a sort. Well, never mind; but someday, you may recall my words. And perhaps..." And then, almost by way of explaining, he added, "As something of you has become part of me. I have not forgotten your tale of Pouch and his wretched companions at

129

Goosepastures. Come what may, here too a few Americans have always been ready, aye ready (if you will allow the fancy). When the Call comes (you understand)."

'Oh no need to go on about it, I told him. Americans made a bigger song about that claptrap than we did. And God only knew, I'd spent long hours squeezing out patriotism like toothpaste from that ridiculous book Moskvin had foisted on me — ("Listen my children and you shall hear of the midnight ride of Paul Revere, stopping over, no doubt, to look in on Barbara Frietche and John Brown's body en route to Concorde Bridge").

'I still was sore at losing that teaching job. Well, we all have our professional pride.

' "The ritual fables! Can you possibly have swallowed those shop-soiled clichés!" he exclaimed (and I really do believe that he was astonished). "People must be told something but, stranger as you are, surely, surely . . . Ours was no revolution. It was privilege against privilege, masterclass against masterclass.

' "Come, Gidner, you have a sharp enough eye. To your credit, you have sought definitions for your definitive work (which I suspect will never be completed). Liberty! Freedom! The Franchise! What have they to do with these homesteaders scratching for survival? You have seen them uprooted, drifting across the land like dust from the fields that once were theirs. You have glimpsed the despair in their faces, guessed at the sickness in their hearts.

' "And the fear, my dear chap, fear with its many faces."

'He waved his hand vaguely at the stricken land-scape.

' "And you, my dear fellow? My cashier tells me that you have closed your account. You have done with us. Ah, but have we done with you? You came here of your free will. You could have stayed at home. There was no compulsion to live amongst us. But now you are here. True for only a couple of days – but still here. There still may be time enough for a glimpse of our darker places."

'He began to laugh again.

'And I remember thinking, All this is like listening to – well, Mozart's 40th for instance. Everything prattling pleasantly away, all going along nicely, this answering that, that echoing this. Till you think, Why can't life be like this? Urbane, orderly, even elegant? Then, without a breath of warning, a drum roll, a clash of chords, bleak foreboding and a chill at the heart.

'Well, we left it there, turned south once more and, when Farewell spoke again, were back on Oxbow and near the house. "Now, Gidner, tomorrow is Inde-pendence Day when all true Yankees toast a prospect of prosperity and plenty. And here in Palisades our County Fair marks that Glorious Day. It would be intolerable if you should leave us without witnessing such invigorating local manifestation of a nation's pride. It concludes with a splendid fireworks display.

' "You also will see our Great Man from Washing-ton, D.C., a man of the people who comes amongst us so that all may see that he is a man of the people. Furthermore, should naught else stir your breast, you will be overjoyed to know that I am returning to you a rebate on the rent which you have paid during your stay beneath my rooftree." And he handed me a handful of bills.

' "Rebate!" I exclaimed. "But this must be my rent for the entire year."

' "You have paid your dues in kind," he said, laughing again. "Provided me with a second home, as it were. And doubtlessly, there have been times when you have thought (bitterly?) that you were over-charged. Let me do this small thing – I should not like you to leave us supposing that our friendship has been by some sordid arrangement. (And, by the way, larkspur essence is good for crabs.)"

'Then, unaccountably, he tapped me affectionately on a shoulder, giggled again and sloped off to his room and his books. I trailed in after him. "I think William Shakespeare suits the day and the day William Shakespeare" – (he may well have been talking to himself) – and reached for his *Lear*. (He was a well-read old codger; I'll say that for him.) Even as he dropped into that battered old armchair (the horsehair coming out in tufts), he was muttering (oh, I'm not likely to forget),

> "In cities mutinies, in countries discords, in palaces treasons,
> And the bond crack't twixt son and father,
> Ruinous disorders follow us disquietly to our graves."

'Then the book slid to the floor; he hadn't opened it. He was asleep. Amazing!

'Do you know what hit me and like a hammer? That first day came back, the day I'd met him, and the queer feeling in the pit of my stomach that something was happening that I didn't want to happen.

'And not knowing what.'

The County Fair is Palisades' great day and, all morning, the surrounding district had been emptying itself into town, leaving its tributary villages, Smolensk, Christiana, Dundee, Frankfurt, Ceazer, to their sick and dying. On farms scattered across the plains only barn doors creaking in the light airs, tethered dogs howling and tumbleweed scurrying across yards disturbed the stillness. And the railroads brought in folk from as far afield as Pierre, Huron, even Sioux Falls, until twenty thousand folk were crammed into the Fairground, a grassy flat bounded by two groves and the river.

The Farewell house had emptied too and dealt its residents around the State to spend Independence Day with families and friends. At 9.30, Becky was picked up by Bosey Swatt, at 10 o'clock, Henry Farewell, pausing briefly on the porch for a word with Ed Murray, drove off south along Oxbow. Half an hour later Mrs Murray and the children were taken away by a farm neighbour. And George Gidner bicycled off to Silver Creek, three miles beyond the town's limits, to make his final drawing, a breaking-plough that a Mr Christensen still found houseroom for.

At 11.30, an unmarked van slipped quietly alongside the rooming house. Two patrolmen already were at the rear door as Police-Chief Gorkev and a third officer burst into Murray's duplex. A single shot passed harmlessly through the roof. Then the young farmer, arms pinioned, was loaded like a sack and driven off. (Mrs Turton, by her murphy-bed, saw all this coming and going with interest but without alarm.)

It was yet one more blue cloudless day in a long succession of blue cloudless days and George spent it in the company of a couple too old to care to leave their home for even a few hours. And he often declared it to have been the most tranquilly happy day of his Dakota Year. 'The prairie, you know that was the only America I really cared for. Perhaps because now I could picture it as it once had been, a vast spread of buffalo grass where (if you follow me) humans dwelt on sufferance. Frankly, it's the only America I want to remember. And (going back to that day with that old couple, the Christensens) heavens, the utter content of quiet talk as we ate the lunch that they would have me share. Then sitting in a cottonwood grove measuring up, then drawing that plough and then an ox-yoke and then measuring up a claim-shanty. The calm before the storm!

'Because when, in the early evening, I got back to town, the place was seething. No, not just the Fair-ground. Downtown itself. There was no getting through to the house because, at Oxbow and First, the road was blocked, jampacked with people either yelling their heads off or clamped into an unnatural silence. The Settlers' Bank seemed to be the hub of the trouble so I propped that girl's bike against the Rialto Theater's front and pushed across till I could see the bank door had been forced and that folk were either struggling to get in or get out.

'Then I saw Stavros, the same chap who'd first shown me what I was in for from the Homesteader roof. I shouted at him but he looked blankly at me: I might as well have been a store-dummy. But when I persisted, like a zombie he held out a printed sheet,

ALL THE BAROMETERS OF BUSINESS
POINT TO A YEAR OF PROSPERITY.
LET THE SETTLERS' BANK MAKE
YOUR MONEY WORK FOR YOU.

'Only then did I get the hang of things; the bank had gone bust and that ridiculous flimsy was all that the poor devil had salvaged from his savings. Then he jerked from his daze. "They say he's given the lot away," he said quite softly. "You're Hen Farewell's buddy, the Englishman. You know where he's hiding out." And I knew then that this was no place for me. Mercifully, there was an almighty crash and Farewell's Store window fell in. (The astonishing thing was that, until then, no one had made the connection.) Then in they went, the first lot pushed screaming into the jagged glass, as the next wave, Stavros amongst them, trod them down, grabbing anything they could lay hands on. I saw one grandpa stagger out dragging a perambulator loaded with ice-skates. And women and men fought each other for radios, stationery, lingerie, dolls, the lot.

'Anyway, I circled three blocks to come back to Oxbow, ditched the bike and hung about under trees on the opposite side of the highway. If I'd needed confirmation of the bank's collapse, it was here: the rooming house bulged with violence, people prising themselves in and out. Then some ape began tossing

135

books through a smashed window. They landed on the sidewalk and the highway like those dead birds dropping from the sky that day of the duck-hunt. One book thudded at my feet, its elegant gold-tooled spine gaping – Fielding's *Tom Jones*. (I felt like strangling somebody.) I stuffed it into my pocket. (And still have it.) Ye Gods, I tell you I was in a blind panic by this time, never felt so adrift in my life. I remember thinking, Well at least I have my passport and there's the money. But naturally I should have liked my mac, my better suit and my gamp. And there was my primum opus (my only opus), the *Founding Fathers*: I'd worked damned hard on that.

'Then and don't ask me why (because there's no rational explanation) I felt that I had to tell Henry Farewell what was going on, warn him they were in lynching form, etc. Well, I owed him (as they say). I simply couldn't have sloped off. According to his lights he'd been quite decent towards me. I mean to say – returning my rent! Anyway, as likely as not he'd be at the Fair and I might get to him before the news spread there. What a day!

'I paid my dollar and, almost at once, was shoved and heaved along the Fairway like a log in a torrent. Christmas shopping in Oxford Street was nothing to it. Quite indescribable! Then, at a crossing, I spotted Gorkev and a patrolman; they were standing on the roof of a squad car, scanning the crowds. I ducked too late and, when I looked again, Gorkev was alone. They were looking for Farewell and, like Stavros, had fixed on me.

'It was crazy but it was alarming. I mean to say – there was I, twenty-four hours from getting away

136

from the ghastly place and this had to happen, the town buzzing like a maddened swarm of bees. Anyway, I heaved my way outwards until I was squeezed like a pip into a tented backwater where a small band of Americans had gathered around a tall gent who was gazing abstractedly through steel-rimmed spectacles at a large stuffed horse.

' "Ummmmmm," this man was saying, "this indeed is a most moving occasion and" (noticing me) "now that the Gentleman of the Press is here . . ."

'He removed a straw boater from his snowy locks and vaguely shook it at a rock bear penned in a squirrel cage, a sample case of fancy corncobs, a card display of arrowheads and, finally, at the moulting steed.

' "We are gathered here" (staring wildly at the mob heaving past) "to dedicate this noble creature, this steed, sole survivor (above ground that is) of General Custer's Glorious Last Stand." (He was getting a lot of competition from the almighty din around us and repeated this – but with diminished confidence.) "This cavalry mount (when alive) was come upon grazing peacefully upon that bloody field and stabled in honourable retirement by our U.S. Army." (He consulted a small card lodged in his cuff.) "On the occasion of its demise, the cadaver was stuffed by public subscription and for forty years has lain (or stood) in a Pierre repository. A furniture store? I have not been told why this was so." He trailed off dispiritedly and both he and the rest of us leaned forward to peer suspiciously at the mangy beast. Its hide had rubbed off in several places and there was a tainted smell.

' "Ah yes . . ." he went on. "It is incomplete. Of course."

'A businesslike man from the Chamber of Commerce tripped forward. "Here, Mr Vice-President, sir," he said briskly. "This here is what you are looking for." He twitched off some sacking to reveal a waxwork Indian lying face downwards and, with a clever knee-lift, hoisted the effigy into a ludicrous crouch upon the horse's back.

' "We sadly failed to obtain a facsimile U.S. cavalryman of the period . . ." (The V.-P. again consulted his card with some disbelief.) "But the Vogler Saloon and Cigar Store on 4th and Adams has donated this Indian surplus to its business requirements, it having been modernized. The store, of course. The horse's name is Toby. Did I mention this earlier? It is my proud privilege to dedicate Toby. For your children's children . . ."

'We applauded respectfully.

' "Now Mr Little Cloud, if you will kindly step forward . . ."

'The ancient Sioux, last seen at Wounded Knee, shuffled his feet and began to drone. He looked neither at horse nor rider. There was no thunder of hoofs; the fire had gone from him. Another Indian bearing a feathered staff stood by and, when a longer silence indicated that no more might be expected of Mr Little Cloud, this man began to tap a small drum. Two crones huddling like old sacks in a corner of the booth stirred themselves and, uttering pathetic bird-calls, began to hop around the tableau.

'Then a gross woman pushed in, dragging a couple of overfed brats over my feet. "Bang! I gottim," one

138

monster yelled. Perhaps Mr Little Cloud didn't hear: I hope not. The old boy gazed stonily at our pink faces and then, embarrassingly, at me. I've often wondered since then if he knew that I wasn't one of them. Well, I shall never know because from the corner of an eye, I swear that I saw Henry Farewell being jostled along the Fairway. So I trod my way backwards into the mob.

'That County Fair must have been the only place in Dakota where a man could lose himself and I thought that, if I had lost Farewell, then everyone else was going to find it hard to lay hands on him. Grudgingly I admired his good sense in coming where most folk hailed from elsewhere and so had no stake in his collapsed bank. Frankly, tossed about in this flood, I felt quite unnerved and, glimpsing a gap, pushed through and found myself with two others in an exhibition put on by the State Historical Society – a Connestoga wagon, the Verenderaye lead tablet, panels of fading photographs, that sort of thing. And there, confronting its custodian, was Becky. Well, I thought, maybe there's more in your stupid wilful head than I supposed and made to ask her if she had seen her dad. She ignored me.

' " 'Centric, jus' eccentric! Goddammit, what is this junk? Well then for godsake, don' tell me: it's a sledge."

' "A breaking-plough, miss," the man said curtly. (He was a highly respected farmer from Spink County.)

' "Ya pushed it! Holy Pete, them old-timers musta been Tarzans."

' "It was hauled by a yoke of oxen, miss: the farmer guided it."

139

' "Ya don' say! Couple cows, ya mean?"

' "Oxen," the man said.

' "Don' get that oxen gimmick. Say again?"

' "It is a kind of bull."

' "Then call it a bull, for godsake."

' "It is not a bull," he said doggedly. "It is a bull that has – well, sort of lost out."

' "Ya mean it! Don' dig, eh? His doll don' spark him off, eh?"

' "Miss, you go ask your pa. Or maybe this young fellow right behind you will put you to rights. Say, I'm about to shut down this show. Got to escort the Vice-President to the railroad depot and see him aboard 777."

' "No sex-life, ha! Ya kidding!'

' "You seen all you want to see?" the farmer asked abruptly.

'Becky turned. If she was astonished to meet me there, she didn't show it. "He don' appreciate me, Mr Gidner. I swear it. Say, mac, you on this County's payroll? My dad's a very considerable taxpayer. C'm on – information!"

'The man's eyes brightened. "You care to see an ox-yoke, miss?" he asked.

' "Might as well goddammit."

'He touched a massive double yoke, rudely adzed from a walnut tree branch.

' "Care to see how they fixed it?"

' "Ya let any ol' body?"

'He looked around theatrically. "Nobody but you and him here?" he asked softly. "No more 'n minute, mind you. I got my job to watch out for."

' "Ya mean I'd be the first?"

' "Cep' an ox."

'With deceptive ease he hoisted the yoke from its hook and, tossing a rope over a beam, hitched one end. "Now bend your pretty neck, miss, and poke your head through this bent stick loup."

'The yoke settled; he notched the collar until her head was trapped. Then, releasing his hold on the rope, he walked swiftly from his tent.

' "Jeez, this crazy thing's some heavyweight," she complained. "It's damnigh breaking my neck. Thanks, mister; I'll come out now."

' "He's gone," I said. "There's only me here now. Listen, I have to find your father."

' "Remove this thing," she hissed.

' "Have you seen him?"

' "No godammit. Ya crazy? How should I see him here when he's out at Pollocks Crossing. Now you hear me. Get me outa here."

'(Of course! Why hadn't I guessed. He'd be safe there with Ardvaak.) I was off the hook. As for Becky, if I'd had my way, she would have been fitted with an ox-yoke the minute I first clapped eyes on her.

'When I left, the ox's head was buried in straw and uttering muffled grunts. Outside, a mighty organ was blasting, "Life is just a bowl of cherries" and I was still drifting aimlessly around the fairways when darkness fell. Now and then, from the shadow of a tented alley, I glimpsed familiar faces caught in harsh slashes of light – Swatt, Wipf, Visconti, Silver . . .

'("Life is just a bowl of cherries. Life is just . . .")

'My arm was grabbed. It was the Delectable Mountain, Hetty Jo, a helmet festooned with glass grapes flattening her yellow hair, a V-necked jumper moulded snugly around her breasts and, over-all, looking tremendously respectable. "Hi, Gidner!" she bawled. "In here!" and yanked me into a tented diner. "Shan't be seeing you around no mo', no mo'. Hen neither. Got me a job teaching school in California. Go-ahead burg by name of Apricot Grove. You fired: me hired. That's the way the cherries bite."

'I was incredulous. And said so.

' "Oh, Hen penned me one corker of a testimonial. Promised school boards things you'd not believe. Me neither. Had the lot 'cept gold lettering. Well and I guess I got all the answers right on that form they sent me,

Is your voice pleasantly soothing?
AFFIRMATIVE/NEGATIVE/UNAPPREHENDED
Do you see teaching as life-service or life-sentence?
Do you believe Abraham Lincoln did more for the United States than St Paul?"

'She went off into peals of laughter. "I'll skip the other ninety-seven," she giggled. "I guess you lied yourself into a job also, Gidner.

' "And say, Hen gave me that cute square teapot I was saving for. Better a teapot than nothing.

' "Say, you an' him – wadja yak about? Never could poke it outa Hen. Could be you and him was working on how he could empty that bank of his, eh?"

'At any other time, I couldn't have taken her seriously. But this wasn't Any Other Time and I protested vehemently that it wasn't like that at all, that Conversation had been my rent rebate – and hadn't she had a similar arrangement (in a less than upright level of activity)?

' "But wadja yak about?" she persisted.

' "You wouldn't understand," I yelled. "But all right then – Was I a churchgoer back in England? Our parson – what did he look like? Yes, I know it sounds crazy, crazy, crazy. If the parson lived alone as I'd told him, how did he go on for eating/laundry/cleaning? If he was so filthy, why didn't his church fire him? Did he drink tea or coffee?"

' "Well, which did he?" she giggled. "And was it from a square pot? Now why would Hen want to know that creepy stuff? Jeez, if he's emptied a hundred banks I'll root from his corner. But boy, was he one big booby. And all those long-winded bores on his bookshelves!'

'She was a marvellous girl. Do you know, fed up with America as I was, I think if she'd have given me the nod, I'd have gone off with her to California. So I decided, hell, Hetty Jo, you rate a decoration and fished out my grandma's jet brooch (I plainly would never get to Idaho) and pinned it on her V-neck. "Ya mean it?" she squealed. "Say it's real cute. Ya wonderful, Gidner!"

'(I like to suppose that out there in Apricot Grove she's still young and beautiful and that it still adorns her. And I like to think that she teases her husband, "No, for the five-hundredth time, I won't tell you how I came by it.")

'Anyway, there we stood gaping soppily at each other. "Come Fall and I'll be in pretty good shape out there in Calif," she cried. "Ripe an' swellin' like one of their damn apricots. Hey, tell Hen I looked in to say Cheeribye . . ." She pushed her face at me, locked me in her iron embrace and we kissed. "Hey,"

143

she shouted, "I all but forgot – the mailman dropped this letter in at the store. It's for you."

'Then she was gone. That day was becoming more and more absurd. And I recall wondering if there really could be an Apricot Grove. Then I was back on Midway and, trapped in its glare, Dr Swatt was yelling at me. Then he too was carried off, fought his way back and, tripping over ropes and pegs, was gripping my arm and staring crazily up at me.

' "Henry Farewell . . . they'll tear him apart."

' Once more he was buffeted from me, his mouth still opening and closing.

' ". . . well, technically lent it I suppose." (Plainly I'd missed some of it.) "But who lends money on the security of farmland these days! That's *giving*."

'His eyes gleamed.

'How odd, I thought, Swatt's usually such a calm chap.

' "So he's given away the lot," he yelled. "They say there's nothing left but the fixed furniture. He must be loco.

' "I've lost twelve thousand myself."

'He grabbed my wrist.

' "Twelve thousand! Cut you in, eh?"

'Cut me in! It was preposterous. In his right mind, Swatt couldn't possibly have considered it.

' "No," I shouted. "He rented me a room. That store job – well, he had to hire summer help, didn't he. Couldn't stand him. And that's the truth. Wish to God I'd never set eyes on him."

'It was a crude denial.

'I felt terrible.

'And he didn't believe me. And I was afraid.

144

'Then, and I don't know how, I found myself under brilliant white floodlight at the gates. Beyond lay a shadow-land of trees and I was pushing my way to their shelter when Gorkev pinned my arms.

'His eyes glinted. And he grinned. He didn't need to speak.

'I jerked up his arms, kneed him hard in the crutch and ran.

'And I remember this going round and round in my head, "I can't hang on till tomorrow. It's got to be tonight. Tonight!"'

George Gidner cautiously skirted downtown and, keeping well clear of the Mobilgas station's red flashing lamp, only crossed Oxbow when he was sure that the rooming house was empty. Groping in darkness from the porch door, stumbling across overturned furniture, he guessed at the devastation. Then he tripped over the collapsed Coney Island deckchair and went down heavily; the dish of artificial fruit exploded beneath him. As he rose, feet tangled in a muddle of clothes, coathangers chimed against his face.

This was impossible. He switched on the light.

Now he could see the case and, sweating with anxiety, flung it open upon the bed and dredged up a shirt and his second suit from the litter. Then he turned back to the switch.

A foot turned up a scatter of papers. Gidner's *Founding Fathers of Teddy County*. Beside himself with sheer funk he began scooping and scraping them into the suitcase.

An automobile drew up. And another and another.

145

He sprang across the mess, slammed the door, slid its bolt and made for the side window. But, even as he pushed at the sash, the door was kicked in.

Grunting like a trapped animal he lowered his head and bullocked into the intruders. They gave before him and he might have driven clear into the foyer had not the deckchair tripped him for a last time. Down he went.

He shoved his hands across his face. They were dragged off. He was struck and kicked again and again.

Barely conscious, he heard a voice screaming into his face, 'Where is he? Farewell! Where's that bastard Farewell?'

That's Hadtlestadt, he thought. Hadtlestadt!

He was hauled to his feet. They pinned his outstretched arms to a wall. He was slapped again and again, then viciously punched in the pit of his stomach.

And that was Hadtlestadt also.

He kicked out: his attacker screamed and collapsed.

But another jumped in. He felt his nose give. It was Amunsden, the amiable coach.

He knew then that he was going to be sick. 'Pollocks Crossing!' he retched. 'He's there. You'll find him at Ardvaak's Store.'

It was passed on, shouted to men in the waiting cars. 'Pollocks Crossing! He's holed up at the Crossing.'

Then they left.

He crawled to the window and, as he vomited, remembered how Hadtlestadt had stood there in the early morning darkness, inviting him to join the duck-hunt. And now it was a man they were hunting. What had gone wrong? He had been half in love with this land. Then, for a crazy moment, it seemed that the banker was at his elbow and murmuring, 'We are not to be relied upon, my dear fellow. Shake the sack and dangerous men may come tumbling out.'

They're savages, he thought bitterly. Scratch skin-deep and . . . His face, reflected in the pane, completed the sentence.

His limbs ached and, dragging himself to the bed, he pressed his bloody face into it and, for a long time, lay panting. Then he limped to the mirror and, strapping plaster across his broken nose, stared at a stranger.

It was high time to go but he turned again for a last look at his small corner of a country he was about to quit. Pages of his book lay scattered around the floor and he tipped their fellows amongst them. He wanted no part of this people and, giving substance to his shame and anger, he hurled the deckchair at the window. Stubborn to the last, it shattered the glass but jammed the frame.

From the gloom of no-man's-land, a voice by the murphy-bed drawled, 'When are you going to pay your War Debts, young man? Have a nice day.'

Great heavens, she was still there.

A man was coming up the porch steps. It was Ed Murray. Each stared aghast at the other's wrecked face. 'They couldn't knock it out of me,' the young farmer muttered. 'But I'll not forget.'

'You're mad. Every last one of you!' George Gidner spat it. 'Get out of my road.' He snatched up his mac and umbrella, roughly shouldered the farmer aside and ran down the porch steps into the dark and deserted street.

As he approached the railroad depot, a patrol car was leaving for downtown. Behind the driver, he glimpsed the Vice-President.

Locomotives were being switched for the long haul and, choosing a seat facing east, he lay back and closed his eyes. Perhaps he recalled his last train journey when, half-hesitant, half-hopeful, he had his first stunned sight of a landscape he had come to know so well. Even to love. Perhaps he recalled the nameless girl who had so charmed him and who now would never know how he had lived his Dakota year. Perhaps the day, with its denial and betrayal, had been too much for him so that he thought of nothing at all.

777 uttered a deep-throated bellow, clanged its bell, blew a towering column of steam into the night, shuddered and dragged itself off towards Chicago.

*　　　*　　　*

'Do I consider that Henry Farewell was a remarkable man?

' "Remarkable"! That can mean anything. He was a romantic, if that means he lived life second-hand. And he was a silly man. But he wasn't mad, if that's what you are getting at.

'By Jove, how I'd love to hear your report to the Chamber of Commerce! I can guess what you'll tell them about him. But what will you say about me?'

'I have come here,' Henry Farewell said gravely, 'because I have nowhere else to go. Those who gave an undertaking did not turn up at Oates's place and Sarah Oates begged me to leave – her man evidently was too ashamed to put in an appearance. The word has got around that Ed Murray had been arrested by Gorkev and our plans knocked out of the poor fellow. And the barrier where we planned to halt the Vice-President's train and make him listen . . . those manning it must surely have heard the same tale and abandoned their posts.'

He did not speak for a few moments. Then he said, 'But I have given it away. The money. Thirty-six farmers will receive cancellation of their mortgages and loans by tomorrow's mail.'

'The lot?' Mr Ardvaak asked casually.

'In modern banking, it only is possible to dissipate certain assets. But I did what I could to clean out the cupboard. I sold the Store and Rooming House to the Bank and so on. I came away with nothing but the clothes I stand in and this.' He nodded towards his bassoon.

They sat in silence.

'Ed Murray . . .' Mr Ardvaak said. 'They're wrong. Depend upon it, Gorkev and his monkeys'll get nothing outa him.

'And you running . . . No sense to it. Might just as well sit it out in my backroom. Give it a couple of days to simmer down and I'll send word to Sheriff Findlayson. Till then bet your bottom dollar it won't be just him on his lonesome looking for you: the Law will get all the cooperation it can use tonight. Blow a head off and half a dozen kin will scream blue murder whilst rest of us wait to read it in *The Plow*. But money!'

'Do not reproach me,' the banker said. 'Believe me, after serving at its altar these many years, I feel like a lapsed priest; it is not an easy feeling.'

Mr Ardvaak began to laugh softly. 'Outside story books, who'd believe it. Have not forgot . . .' He touched his eyes. 'How could I? Out here on this half-section. Watching the trees and crops burn up and Ella die. Finance Corporation moving in to repossession everything. 'Cept despair. They left me that. No, ain't forgot. It's Dollars we live by.'

Neither spoke.

'Going to be a long night,' Mr Ardvaak said. 'How about one of your stories, Henry? That time in England. Great hand at tale-telling: surely will miss you if they put you in the pen.'

'What a satisfying compliment,' the banker said. 'Occasionally, it has crossed my mind that I was better suited to occupations other than finance. Perhaps I should have tried my hand at one of the performing arts: Politics perhaps or the Church? Well then, I shall tell you (and mind, only because you have asked me) of the chap who made the deepest impression on me Over There. You will find it a most remarkable instance of the past foretelling . . . no, foreshadowing the future.

'He was a vicar. But that title is too impersonal, even officious. They have another name . . . yes, of course, "parson". Really "person", James. The English are unusually skilful at disguising deference owed their betters. They could not very well call their spiritual director "mate", "chum" or "duck" when, the next Sunday, he would be offering them the solemn mystery of the Host. So they called him "that person".'

'How come you met up with this guy?'

'This person, this parson, was ministering to a remote parish in a northern county, no more than a scatter of cottages and farms in grey stony country, a place to which no one came unless he had business there. Recall the sage deserts of Idaho. People them with a folk speaking an archaic mode of our tongue, much akin to King James's Bible, full of "thees" and "thous".

'It was such a country as that.

'Now, see me alight from a rural bus, a ramshackle contraption, fellow travellers eyeing me with an amalgam of curiosity and hostility, then, my ears still jangling with thees and thous, surveying the scene before me. With emotion. For, James, this was the place where my family, the Farewells, had lived out generation after generation, each one passing a tithe of his breed to his sons and they to their sons, as my father passed something of himself and them to me.'

He paused meditatively, before resuming with renewed eloquence, 'The bus moved off, I climbed a roadside bank, went through a squealing gate and there I was – in the burial yard of my family's parish.'

' "The parish"?' Mr Ardvaak murmured, savouring it.

'Yes, the parish – a parcel of ecclesiastical land – and more dead than quick peopled it. That yard was fat with folk, one laid upon another: the sexton's spade must have cleft an earlier tenant each time he bedded a new one. Few there will rise incorruptible.

'Yet it was a pleasant place, an untutored garden. And though the roots of stones marked the dead like shadows, their heads rose like finger-posts amongst herbage – old man's beard, willow herb, sowthistle and fleaweed.'

(Mr Ardvaak nodded appreciatively and, stepping delicately amongst the carved stones and between parting grass and flowers, followed.)

'At once, on the instant, I felt myself at home. There were Farewells everywhere. And, James, need I say that I was not a little proud that my forebears had not stinted their purses. Whereas the Platts, the Hennings, a multitude of Smiths and such fry, made do with no more than a date and a name, the Farewells had celebrated their going with winged cherubs, urns and hour-glasses, a catalogue of necrophilic decoration.

'I made a nodding acquaintance with Dorcas Farewell, Amelia Ann, Isaac, Malachi Farewell. Even an Endymion Farewell. Endymion! I lost myself. And why not? These – as they say Over There – were my kith and kin, and never before had I attended so thronged a family party. If, then and there, they had risen around me, I knew in my bones that they would have known me as one of them.'

'Never doubt it,' Mr Ardvaak murmured. 'Years and miles are nothing to the dead. It is another world.'

'And there were stones worn away by weather,' the banker cried enthusiastically. 'Many of these also must have been Farewells. And, before that, in days when memorials had not been thought of, those of my people known only to God.

' "Known only to God"! Though sadly I am not a believer, it is a sentiment which I much approve. So, not inappropriately I feel, I uttered those immortal lines (and in quite a loud voice),

> Each in his narrow cell forever laid,
> The rude forefathers of the Farewells sleep.

You recall the rest. No? Well do not equate "rude" with its current usage.'

He fell into a long silence whilst the storekeeper noisily scraped out his pipe before refilling with Prince Albert Ready Chopped. 'Not as I recall,' he said regretfully. 'Miss Emily never had us learn that one. Many a one but not that one. Kids learn nothing in school these days. Nothing to last 'em out. Oughta hire teachers like Miss Emily. Say, that parson?'

'Ah yes. Then I visited with the parson and, even now James, I see that poor fellow as though he had joined us here. In years, he was over the hill and well down the other side. And he was no flashy dresser. Anything but.

'Had his flock been folded in these United States, he would have been fired within the month. There were more buttons missing from his waistcoat than secured it. And from this same garment, one would not need to be a Sherlock Holmes to identify meals he had lately eaten.'

'A loner!' Mr Ardvaak murmured.

'But the poor fellow made me more than welcome. I scarcely had broached the purpose of my visit before he cleverly balanced a tin kettle on a spirit stove whilst telling me that this same earthenware teapot had served him at Queen's, Oxford (which place numbered also as alumni the great Milton, Wordsworth and the assassin Felton). "It is most unusual for a pot in daily use to last so long," he told me. "And, over the years, antiquity has added a *je ne sais quoi* to each mashing."

'And James, like you he was a pipe smoker. Even whilst mashing the tea, he gouged a sodden gobbet from his pipe's bowl with a scissor blade. Part he swept back into his pouch and part fell into the pot. Then he said . . .'

(Mr Ardvaak unflinchingly readied himself for the tea.)

'Then he said, "Ah! A banker! And how, pray, do you propose to enter into the Kingdom?"

'Well, this took me aback. It is not customary for our Palisades ministers of religion to suggest that who dies rich, dies disgraced, relying (as they must) for their stipends falling from rich men's tables.

'But I answered that, in my bones, I knew that I should die a poor man. And to this, he remarked that such a choice was offered to all men; we could rid ourselves of encumbrance. Even with joy. For, at our ends, it would be so.

'Then we spoke of God (although you must understand, James, that their English God is not so dominant a business institution as is ours). And then . . . and then he seemed to forget me whilst he sucked, turn and turn about, his pipe and his teacup.

'And when he spoke again, it was to say that many men live without heed of their ends. "Carry on" was the phrase he used. "We carry on as if we had Forever. Sunday after Sunday, my own people, here in this parish of Oxgodby give Eternity the wink and nod. 'Do good whilst ye yet have time,' I call out (as the Book of Common Prayer charges me). And they bawl back 'Amen!' even though I have told them times beyond number that its meaning is 'I agree'.

' "Then, let us suppose that I preach on the text, *What shall it profit a man if he gain the whole world and lose his own soul?* A most solemn proposition if ever there was one! And, as they sidle past me on their way back to the rest of the week, they mumble, 'Varry nice sermon tha treated us to, Parson. Ah took in ivverey word tha uttered. Aye, varry nice! An' thou'rt danged reet.'

' "And their offerings come to a few shillings and coppers.

' "Last week, I visited my old school on its Speech Day and the lads sang their heads off,

> Time like an ever-rolling stream
> Bears all its sons away.

but, until they draw their last breath, in their hearts, they will protest, 'Ten thousand shall fall. But not

155

me, not me.' If I stood in my pulpit each Sabbath
Day left to me and cried, 'Your end is nigh. The hour
of your dissolution is at hand. It is Now or Never.'
Still they would not believe. They would bleat, 'Amen!
And thou'rt danged reet, Parson.' "

'Then the old man leaned and put a nicotined
finger on my arm. (You know, James, how I cannot
bear to be touched: to my shame I drew back.) And
he said, "Ah, my American friend, you are not a
believer. That I can see. But no matter – do good
whilst you have yet time." '

Henry Farewell stopped and shivered slightly.
'Even repeating words spoken at such distance and in
such a place, gives me an odd uneasiness. As if
someone was walking on my grave.'

For a time the two sat in the gathering darkness.
Lamps glowed dimly in windows of far-off farms. A
star appeared. The blind man was first to stir; he
moved confidently towards the open door. 'It was a
good tale, Henry,' he said. 'Saw it plain as daylight.
That bit about his pipe and his teapot . . .

'And he was damned right. Behoves the all of us to
see to it that we die well. Oughta be easy enough.
Living's the hard part.'

For a long time the two friends were silent.

Then, in the darkness, an automobile braked and
halted.

'Ardvaak! This is Sheriff Findlayson. I know that
Mr Farewell is with you. Have him step outside so we
can talk.'

The blind man did not reply but stepped back from
the open door and, reaching below his counter for a
shotgun, said, 'Grab a hold of this.'

The banker took it doubtfully and moved forward. 'Do not approach, Sheriff,' he called, peering into the blackness. 'I am armed and my regrettable record with guns is common knowledge.'

Mr Ardvaak smiled.

'Now see here, Mr Farewell, you don't need telling I don't care for this business. But a warrant has been sworn out in town and my job is to execute it. Let's go back to Palisades.'

'No,' the banker said firmly. 'And how did you learn that I might be found here?'

'Mob knocked it out of the Englishman.'

'Ah yes! Poor Gidner! What must he think of us!'

'Mr Farewell, sir, it's for your own safety. You must know that. I have sealed off the road. O.K. then. Not Palisades. If we get going now I can move you down to Pierre till folks come to their senses.'

Henry Farewell did not reply.

'O.K., then you know how it is. I'm coming to take you.'

A shotgun roared.

'Nothing 'gainst you, Findlayson,' Mr Ardvaak yelled. 'Only loosed off so as you can tell that tinhorn slob, Gorkev, there's a heap of ammunition up here. Sell it.'

Footsteps retreated. The car backed, turned and went.

'Now what?' Henry Farewell asked.

'Now what! Now that the Englishman's traded you in, you and me are going out of business. Made your call, Henry, and now must back it. Only one way out. Well then, let's do it proper.

'What's stirring over the bridge?'

The banker crossed the gravel and, from the cannon's plinth, looked across the river. 'If lights mean anything, a great throng of people have gathered on the eastern bluffs. And more are approaching along the Palisades highway.

By this rude bridge that spanned the flood . . .

(We might reasonably claim that the Bitter-root Bridge is ours.)

By this rude bridge that spanned the flood,
Their flag to evening breeze unfurled . . .

(I suppose that Breitmeyer's booster banner still floats above us?)

Their flag to evening breeze unfurled,
Here once the embattled farmers stood . . .

(But James, can we claim to be "embattled farmers"? When the call came, our farmers did not come.)'

Mr Ardvaak cackled. 'Sixty years, if it's a day since I heard them lines. Miss Emily had us learn 'em in 4th Grade. When she'd done with us I guess no kids in these United States could come near us for little patriots. Wed a feller down south, out Pearl Creek way; he run a livery stables in White River. Railroad put him out of business. Lot of pep, that little woman. Couldn't have been a day more 'n eighteen when she taught school. Used to get swept offen her feet. "Freedom was bought dear with our forebears' blood, children. Always mind that," she used to holler. Had bright blue eyes. Flashed sparks when she got mad. Guess she gave her feller a bad time if he didn't measure up.'

And still choking with laughter he joined his friend

158

on the low concrete platform. 'Well Henry,' he said. 'What say we honour her pledge? How did that last line go –

> Here once the embattled farmers stood
> And fired a shot heard round the world.'

And, feeling for the ropes, he began to unlash the tarpaulin shrouding his gun. Then, shoulders to the wheels, they eased it around until its muzzle pointed towards where, below in the darkness, he supposed the bridge to be.

The banker's face lit up. He too laughed. 'Why James, at long last, I really do believe you are going to let me put her through her paces. And how proper an occasion! At a stretch (admittedly a long stretch) this might be described as the last battle of the Revolutionary War. No? Perhaps parties of school-children on educational tour-buses from Back East will be conducted to this site and gather around and, at *their* Miss Emily's command, burst forth,

> "By Pollocks Bridge that spanned the flood,
> Breitmeyer's flag to evening breeze unfurled,
> Here once the embattled Ardvaak stood . . ." '

He paused and stroked the barrel.

'I shall swivel her two degrees to our right. A trifle, no more. There! Now I shall elevate the muzzle by one ratchet. Now! Do you suppose that she will . . . well (in your parlance), work?'

'Work? Course she'll work. Always told me she would damnwell work, ain't you? Prise out that there bung and roll this here ball down her. And I'll bring up the charge and train from my backroom. Best look sharp for fear Findlayson can't stop them city animals getting across. Here, send up this rocket; I got a stock in for the Fourth. Give 'em a fair warning and us a sighting. Reckon you wouldn't care to hit some poor soul. 'Cept maybe Gorkev.'

Despite its proprietor's impatience, Henry Farewell continued to minister reverently to the aged fieldpiece and, only after checking each routine, did he flick his cigar-lighter. 'Even Valley Forge cannot match our Dakota winters,' he said. 'There may well be a hairline crack in the brass. And should that be so, depend upon it, James, she will blow up. And, even if she does not, I cannot vouch for the restraining-chocks holding. So perhaps it would be well if we withdrew.'

He bent, lit the train and hustled back his companion until, tripping over a cuspidor, they fell together into the store.

There was a blinding flash, an almighty roar. For a single theatrical instant, false-front, flag, bluffs, bridge and river were brilliantly lit. And the antique gun reared convulsively, plunged backwards across the gravel, bounded over the porch and, showering shattered glass, ripped a gap in the storefront, then sweeping up the iron stove, crashed through the hardware display, to bury itself deep inside the backroom. The building shuddered. Tools, pans, baths, basins, stoves, buckets, cooking pots banged down from hooks and shelves and a wildly swinging cord snapped to discharge a shower of tin kettles upon the cowering banker. And dust as old as Mr Ardvaak's store mushroomed up and outward.

Then startled silence.

'Great God in Heaven!' Henry Farewell exulted and, blundering through the debris, stumbled to the door. 'We shall never know what its projectile did. But the gun herself was devastating. And I quite definitely glimpsed Breitmeyer's banner.'

  ' "Shoot if you must this old grey head
    But spare your country's flag," she said'

Mr Ardvaak recited but, because his store teeth had slipped, rendering speech intelligible only to himself, he re-aligned them with his thumb to repeat Barbara Frietche's immortal defiance. Then said, 'What's to be seen?'

'Nothing,' the banker replied. 'But something plainly has impressed them – their headlamps have been switched off. Do you suppose that they fear a prolonged cannonade? How sad that we are unable to oblige.'

The storekeeper crawled into the wreckage and felt about the floor.

'Loose off a few more rockets. Might as well use 'em.'

And a couple of minutes later, three rockets spurted into the sky, their starry trails curving lazily across the night to burst in blazing festoons high above the river.

'Well?' the blind man called impatiently.

'The bridge still stands. Ah, yes . . . they are directing a spotlight. A flag! Yes, a flag! And on the highway! Good gracious! There appears to be a man entangled in it. And others are scuttling back up the bluffs.'

'Cool 'em off,' Mr Ardvaak remarked calmly.

161

'Shame that Miss Bull ain't around, Henry. Would have been proud of you. Miss Emily also. She'd have had us singing.' And he began to quaver,

'And the rockets red glare, bombs bursting in air,
  Gave proof through the night that our flag was
    still there.

Say, know what she used really to get mad at? Ploughing! "This here's cattle country," she used t'holler. "Lord God didn't seed buffalo grass so as your dads might rip it up. But Judgement Day'll come. Never doubt it. Mebbe not next week, mebbe not in my time. But in God's good time, this land will turn from farming folk and dry up to dust." '

'Your teacher was a perceptive young woman,' Henry Farewell said. 'We – and they' (gesturing vaguely across to the further bluffs) 'are reaping that whirlwind.'

'Coming over danged solemn the both of us,' the storekeeper said. 'Give us a tune on that horn of your'n. How about "Red River Valley"? Was my old Ma's favourite.'

*   *   *

'Forget? Of course, I should like to forget. But remembering and forgetting can't be turned on and off like the bath-tap.

'I tried once.

'What do I mean? What do you suppose I mean! I mean that I tried retiring from the human race, that's what I mean. You might as well know: everyone else around here does. But they dragged me back and I never had the nerve for a second go.

'Why did I do it? Oh, that's easy. I simply was sick of myself.'

George Gidner's head throbbed. He recalled how often on the road to Ardvaak's store he had watched this same night mail, a glittering string of light racing along the river bluffs. And now, in a few more minutes, it would carry him from Teddy County and, soon, from Dakota. Then Pollocks Crossing, Henry Farewell, this awful day itself, would sink into the past. And, in time, he would forget.

He heard the locomotive's bell jangling wildly, felt brakes grip, wheels grind, 777 slide to a shuddering stop. Unseen by him, a flimsy barrier of hurdles, lit by a couple of red lanterns, had been thrown across the track. He pushed down a window and peered into the night. Even as he watched, rockets bursting in a shower of sparks abruptly revealed the store at the Crossing. And Breitmeyer's banner above it. Then utter blackness.

'Great God!' he muttered through swollen lips.

The heart is stirred in different ways and it would be hard to say whether George Gidner wept or laughed as he abandoned his baggage and, taking

163

only his umbrella to help him across the uneven turf, climbed down to the track and stumbled towards the river.

More than a couple of hundred automobiles were scattered about the grass along each side of the highway. And more were arriving. Half-a-dozen student couples were shuffling to a cracked record on a portable gramophone, stubbornly asserting,

> Life is just a bowl of cherrie–s
> Life is just a bowl of cherrie–s
> Life is just a bowl of cherrie–s . . .

'Now men,' Sheriff Findlayson was calling through a loud-hailer. 'Go on home. Now hear me. Your money is safe.' He waved a telegram. 'You have my word. This here reads TRANSFER OF SETTLERS' BANK FUNDS INVALID. Your dollars is safe as in your pockets. Go on home. Mr Farewell is sick. He don't know what he's been doing. Depend upon it; he'll stand trial. But he's coming back to town in one piece.

'Now any tale about a bunch of farmers shooting up the Vice-President is false.

'He's fast asleep this minute at The Homesteader and there ain't no farmers. They're in their beds like you folks oughta be in your'n. There ain't nobody holed up 'cept old Ardvaak and Farewell. Now go on home.'

Nobody moved.

'Now hear me,' he began again. 'Me and Chief Gorkev here aim to go up and take him. There'll be no shooting. He'll come peaceful. So go on home.'

George pushed through. He's a fair man, he

thought; I trust him. But not Gorkev: he's mean. 'Why can't you leave him, Sheriff?' he called. 'Leave him and let him come back in the morning of his own accord. He'll do that – particularly when he finds that he's done whatever he is supposed to have done for Nothing.'

Findlayson turned curiously towards him, scanning the torn clothes and battered face. 'Now, son, I don't care to do what has to be done. But it's near out of my hands and my job's on the line. Depend upon it: I'll see he gets decent treatment and (between the two of us) he mayn't come to trial.'

'He's a Commie Red,' Gorkev shouted furiously. 'And Reds ain't Americans. Reds is vermin to be put down.'

He turned on George. 'And you and me will be having a little session when I get back to town. Just the two of us, buddy.' (He was still limping.) 'Come on, Findlayson. Let's go take the bastards.'

The other nodded briefly. 'O.K.,' he said. 'But no rough stuff. They're both well-respected men out here in my County. I'll do the talking.'

Two grey trucks ground up the slope, stopped and out tumbled a couple of dozen tin-hatted National Guardsmen, young executives, store managers, a couple of dentists and a doctor. Brisk commands were bawled and these clattered into ranks and banged down the rifle butts. Another command and bayonets were rammed home. Two young women began to clap politely.

Their officer, Harvey Lee Skapiera, a lumber merchant, stamped to a splendid salute before the astounded law-officer and shouted, 'Company 4522 at readiness and reporting for duty.' ('Sir,' he added dubiously.)

'What in hell's name are you doing here?'

'Called out by the Governor, sir.'

'Well, there's no call for you here. One feller's blind and t'other's crazy.'

'Governor's orders, sir.'

He saluted (but less confidently), yelled another command, causing a couple of store-clerks to trot back to the truck, assemble an ancient machine gun, then like a tin-soldier tableau, kneel behind it.

There was an appreciative buzz of excitement; the dancing party broke up and gathered excitedly around. But this was stilled when one struck up,

> Columbia, the pride of the ocean,
> Home of the brave and the free . . .

and hands were bent on breasts, eyes raised to the heavens.

It was stirring stuff.

But that was not all.

Half a dozen automobiles roared up and more men came running. They were sporting quaint fore-and-afts, red bandanas lettered LEGION POST 6598 across their breasts and had armed themselves with deer rifles and shotguns. Their leader was High School Principal Moskvin. This motley throng shuffled into some sort of order whilst Moskvin unfurled the Stars and Stripes on a telescopic steel pole which he probed skyward seeking a breeze. Then, ignoring Lieutenant Skapiera's protests and swerving past the Sheriff's outstretched arms, weapons at the ready, flag flapping, they trotted downhill towards the bridge.

The watching citizens cheered. One cried, 'Well done, the Minutemen!'

And people began to clap.

George watched incredulously.

A tremendous flash of flame from the western bluffs split the night. Then a roar, then an almighty smack, succeeded by echoing chimes as some missile clanged and rattled along the bridge's girders. Then a shocked silence.

A hissing shower of rockets bursting extravagantly in a clatter of explosions revealed the crowd flat on its face and Legion Post 6598 scuttling uphill in disorderly flight, their deserted commander swaddled in his flag and furiously wrestling a way from beneath it.

Sick at heart, he turned away. As people began to rise shakily to their feet to switch off headlamps, he recognized several of his attackers – Amunsden, Stavros, Hadtlestadt. It's not money now, he thought bitterly; they are here because Henry Farewell has perpetrated the unforgivable, the Big Sin – he's dared to be different. They are here to put him down.

He made his way in a wide arc and, now, at the riverside, all was as still as on that long gone afternoon when first he had found his way to the Crossing and Ardvaak's store. Then he heard the banker's bassoon, its low voice mingling with the hidden water's flow, unsung words he would never forget.

> Yet linger awhile e'er you leave us,
> Do not hasten to bid us adieu,
> And remember the Red River Valley . . .

He slipped off his shoes. Then, waist-deep and probing ahead with the umbrella, he began to wade across.

The bassoon's sound abruptly ceased. Ahead and above, where the hidden road climbed the dark shoulder of the bluffs, he heard the rattle of an automatic weapon.

Then a single shot.

They sat on the floorboards, their backs to what was left of the counter. A kerosene stable lantern did no more than nudge away the dark.

'Think of it, James,' Henry Farewell murmured. 'This great land with its Monuments and Inscriptions, its Honoured Dead, its Glory and Fame . . .

'And now our countrymen are hunting us like animals in the night, banker and bank-robber.'

'Not all that out of the way of things,' Mr Ardvaak answered. 'Americans who don't own a bank will like as not rob one. Say – your piece about that parson scraping his pipe into the teapot. Couldn't happen here. In these United States folks have become too damned clean. What hour do you make it?'

'A quarter after midnight.'

'Take 'em a half hour to drive down to Palisades and come up behind us. Less than that if they chance crossing the river higher up. No more 'n hour left at the most.'

'And then?'

Mr Ardvaak considered this. 'Jail or make an end of it. Choice is our'n.'

'I could not bear to be caged like a beast,' the banker said. 'To sit, stand, eat, sleep at the order of some gross bully like Gorkev. Let us consider our options. For instance, what comes afterwards? You follow my line of thought, James?'

168

The storekeeper did not answer immediately. Then he said, 'Dark now, dark then. Feel that way yourself?'

'No, I should not like to suppose myself snuffed out like a candle. I should like to believe . . . well, you recall that old Sioux in our Palisades Courthouse. Like him, I should like to believe that there is a Sisnoyinni. And Beyond It. And Beyond That. Alas, I cannot. And yet I do believe that there may be, that there is something in us that can be without us.'

For a time neither spoke.

'. . . And shall be after us,' he murmured.

Again there was a long silence.

Then the banker said, 'Those lines that I recall quoting to you the day Gidner came to town – by the Englishman, Chesterton. You remember?

> To an open house in the evening
> Home shall men come.

Well, I could settle for that.'

He stood up, instinctively dusting down his suit, then picked a way through the wreckage to the porch.

'It would appear that the County Fair has pulled up its pegs and moved out to the eastern bluffs,' he said drily.

> 'I have seen them in the watchfires
> Of a hundred circling camps

as your mentor, Miss Emily, certainly would have come up with. Listen, someone wishes to parley.'

It was a loud-hailer.

'This is Sheriff Findlayson. I have come across to talk, Mr Farewell. I am unarmed. Switch on a light if you hear me.'

The banker picked up the stable lamp and, returning to the porch, swung it. 'Turn off your headlamps,' he called. 'And leave the automobile. But do not approach the store.'

Both he and their visitor were lost in the darkness.

'Mr Farewell, I beg of you to surrender yourself. You have no chance. Men are coming from town along the west bank. Nobody wants to crucify you. Come on in so you can have medical help. And say – Mr Ardvaak can remain here.'

'You hear, James?' the banker spoke casually over his shoulder. 'They have offered us excellent terms. You heard? I am unwell. Perhaps they will not put me in the Penitentiary. A psychiatric ward! And when I can re-affirm that God's portrait adorns our dollar bill and endorse my claim to sanity by raising a hand and crying "Aye! All's well in the land", then I may be let free to be sniggered at behind my back. I think that I am posing the case fairly to you, James.'

'No!' Mr Ardvaak shouted with unusual vehemence from the store. 'Tell them, No. Me, I've had enough.'

'It will not be easy.'

'I reckon our friend Gidner will find a place for us in his book. Strong sense of duty, that young feller.' Mr Ardvaak laughed sardonically.

'Sheriff, you heard? Thank you for your courtesy in hearing us out.'

'I'm sure sorry it's come to this, Mr Farewell. And you also, Ardvaak. I shall set up road-blocks both sides of you and wait till morning. Feel daylight 'll bring some sense all round. Good night!'

They heard him walk off across the gravel.

The automobile's headlamps blazed.

'Don't move, Farewell.' It was Police-Chief Gorkev. 'One step and I'll gun you down. Stand off, Sheriff. These men are resisting the Law.'

'Ah you!' the banker cried, shielding his eyes against the glare. 'So you have crept up like the jackal you are.'

He turned away. A buzzsaw of automatic fire ripped the building.

And was answered by a single gunshot from the store.

The car's headlamps died: it slashed off in a shower of stones.

Henry Farewell reeled back through the door, whimpering with pain, head rolling in agony. 'It is as I supposed – easier to talk of blood than to shed it,' he groaned. 'Where are you, James?'

There was no answer. And when, once more, his eyes became accustomed to the darkness, he saw his friend, still clutching the shotgun, crumpled on the floor. He bent and held the lantern close to the face. One shocked look at the bloody mask was enough and, lowering himself beside the dead man, he leaned once more against the counter. Blood oozed through his fingers.

'Ah well,' he muttered. 'It may be this is a dream of life. And Ardvaak's dream is over.'

Footsteps approached over the gravel and he heard a familiar voice.

It was George Gidner.

Who gazed dismayed yet awed at the banker's stricken face dimly lit by the lantern. 'My God! Whatever have they done to you?' he breathed. Then, incredulously, 'Who are the Americans?'

'Ah,' Henry Farewell murmured, 'who? Who indeed? Miss Bull weighed us up (as she put it) when she remarked there was something about us that alarmed her.'

A smile like a shadow flickered across the dying man's face. 'But then, she was a person of a rare perception. And poor, ignorant Pollock, all those years ago, he too understood. And moved on. Now Gidner, at last do you understand? Our darker places . . .'

He laboured for breath.

'Gidner, my dear fellow, you must visit Great Minden and tell Miss Bull that I wore the suit I had tailored for Occasions. And dying is a very great occasion . . .'

'Miss Bull? Great Minden?'

Henry Farewell's head bowed upon his chest. 'And you, Gidner, should you not go now?' he muttered. 'Whilst *you* have yet time? In the daylight, they will come to their right minds. But now, in this darkness . . .'

George looked furtively at his pocket watch. In a couple of hours it would be daybreak.

A frightful shudder shook his companion. 'Hang on, old man,' he said gently. 'You'll pull through. You're going to be as right as rain. Someone will turn up and we'll get you to hospital. I shan't leave you. When you're fit again, we shall have that holiday in England you've looked forward to. See us at first-hand at last. Dad and Mum will put you up; you'll see all that we've talked about.'

He folded his tweed jacket and eased it behind the lolling head. The banker did not answer. But a hand fumbled and gripped George Gidner's wrist. Now and then, he shuddered.

There was a long silence.

'Say something,' he muttered.

'What? Say what? What do you want me to say? What is there left to say?'

The simple request flustered George Gidner: he was close to tears.

'It was our . . . arrangement . . . your rent.'

A corner of Henry Farewell's mouth signalled a private smile.

'You must say something whilst I still can hear. But if you find these circumstances too bizarre . . .'

His voice trailed away.

'. . . then say something someone else said.'

George sifted through the mishmash his assiduous grammar school master had compelled him to commit to memory: nothing seemed apt.

At last he faltered, ' "Then said he, Though with great difficulty I have gotten hither, I do not repent me of the trouble I have been at to get where I am." '

'Your author seems to have difficulty expressing himself. Now Fielding would have put it more succinctly,' Henry Farewell whispered. 'Your poor man plainly was denied the advantage of sitting in on your sentence-diagramming sessions. But it makes an interesting beginning. Do go on, old chap.'

' "My marks and scars I carry with me . . ." '

'And?'

It was as if the enveloping darkness spoke.

' "And when the day that he must go hence was come, many accompanied him to the riverside . . ." '

'No, not many. Not on this bank. Only poor blinded Ardvaak. And you. Go on.'

' "So he passed over . . ." ' George Gidner groaned. Hair rose at the nape of his neck. His heart banged away. ' "And . . . something, something . . . (I forget) . . . And all the trumpets sounded for him on the other side." '

Someone was coming.

He heard footsteps scraping across the store's forecourt, then moving softly over the porch planks. 'Now what?' he muttered. 'If Gorkev finds me here even near a weapon, I'm for the pen. And, if I use one, worse.'

He loosened Mr Ardvaak's grip on the shotgun.

'What is it?' Henry Farewell mumbled. 'I won't have them touch me. Ardvaak! James, are you there? Shoot me.'

'No, no, I can't,' George said, greatly agitated. 'But I'll try to hold them off.' He released his wrist, took the gun and crept to the gap in the wall.

'Let me in.' It was Becky's frightened voice.

She slipped past him and knelt by the stricken man. 'Oh Daddy!' she sobbed. 'What have they done to you!'

Another fierce shudder shook him. He seemed to forget her.

'Gidner, I can't see you. Are you still there? Your book, your *Brief Lives* . . . Ardvaak – put him in.'

'And you,' George said, holding up the lantern.

'That I had hope of. Thank you.'

His face twitched, unaccountably reminding George of their first meeting in the Bank.

'What will you say?'

'These things are not easy. Not to me, anyway.' (It was said with a touch of irritation.)

'Try.'

' "Henry Farewell, 18 . . ." I don't know. You must tell me.'

' '79,' the dying man whispered.

' "Henry Farewell, 1879 to . . ." '

'1930.'

' "Henry Farewell, 1879 to . . . affirming a free man's independence . . ." No, no, it is too long a subordinate clause; its drift will be lost.'

'You can tidy it up later.'

' ". . . strove to keep alight the revolutionary flame . . . But the times were against him . . . and set upon by lesser men, he, with James Ardvaak, died at Pollocks Crossing." No, no, "died at the Battle of Pollocks Crossing".'

'You must put in that he was attended by his daughter and by his friend, the Englishman.'

'You have said it, not me,' George groaned. 'I have been a poor sort of friend. All I can say is that I was a stranger and did not understand.'

The lamp flickered and went out.

The wrecked store and its four occupants were wrapped in a profound stillness gathering from the encompassing plains.

'Would it be in order for me to say, "And with him, the Frontier died too"?'

'No.' The banker's voice was no more than a breath. 'There are others. There always will be others. Though we do not know them. They will not let the nation die.'

Beneath a heap of merchandise the party line

telephone began to ring. Three short, one long. It went on and on.

'Oh Daddy,' the girl sobbed. 'Don't go.'

George Gidner struck a match and peered intently at Henry Farewell as though still trying to understand. Then he touched Becky's shoulder.

'He's gone,' he said. 'And we must go too.'

Scamblesby
The Lincolnshire Wolds
4 November 1984

Molesworth
Huntingdonshire
6 February 1985